YEAH, SURE. CHILDREN ARE FLEXIBLE
AND "ADJUSTING BEAUTIFULLY" . . .
YEAH, SURE, GROWNUPS SAY THEY DON'T
WANT TO INFLICT THEIR PROBLEMS
ON INNOCENT CHILDREN, BUT
WHAT DO THEY THINK DIVORCE IS . . .
FUN & GAMES?

RICH KIDS

A young love story

Robert Altman and George W. George
present

RICH KIDS

Trini Alvarado   Jeremy Levy

Terry Kiser   David Selby

Kathryn Walker   John Lithgow

Robert Maxwell   Paul Dooley

Irene Worth

Executive Producer Robert Altman

Produced by George W. George and
Michael Hausman

Directed by Robert M. Young

Written by Judith Ross

A Lion's Gate Production

United Artists

A Transamerica Company

RICH KIDS

A Novel
by

H. B. Gilmour

Based on the screenplay
by Judith Ross

RICH KIDS
A Bantam Book / September 1979

ISBN 0–553–13292–X

Published simultaneously in the United States and Canada

Bantam Books are published by Bantam Books, Inc. Its trade-
mark, consisting of the words "Bantam Books" and the por-
trayal of a bantam, is Registered in U.S. Patent and Trademark
Office and in other countries. Marca Registrada. Bantam
Books, Inc., 666 Fifth Avenue, New York, New York 10019.

PRINTED IN THE UNITED STATES OF AMERICA

DEDICATION

For Jessica Gilmour,
and Jennifer George
who make their parents
    Rich Kids . . .
    With love.

Book One
Rich Kids

Chapter One

Franny Philips had long, thick dark hair which could be coaxed to neatness with loving attention but otherwise tended to overflow the orderly borders of her soft oval face; it was hair that might creep unexpectedly across her pale pink cheeks or fling itself at the will of the wind in several directions at once or even lash out meanly, two or three silken strands at a time, to swat at her dark-rimmed blue eyes.

This morning, though, her hair was being nice to her. It was jittery, but it was waiting with some control, as she was, to find out what was going to happen today. A hank here, a lock there, a couple of stray strands spiraled lazily toward her pursed lips as if to get a better view, a more central position from which

1

to watch the street two stories below where Franny's
sleepy young eyes were focused.

With a yawn that ended in a sigh, Franny brushed
the hair back from her face, rested her head against
the shutters, and curled more deeply into the soft
cushioned corner of the window seat. Her faded pink
flannel pajamas crept up uncomfortably, leaving her
wrists and ankles out in the cold, looking, she thought,
like bluish-white chicken skin. She shifted and tugged
at the rumpled little-girl pajamas, annoyed and a bit
puzzled by how quickly she was outgrowing things
these days.

Across the room, Shag, who was flopped like a mop
at the end of her bed, whined in his sleep. It was a
high-pitched sound, something between a yip and a
growl, and Franny glanced over at him apologetically,
as if to say, don't worry Shag, I'm not outgrowing you.
One of the sheepdog's ears twitched an acknowl-
edgment. Then he rolled over, almost slipping off the
edge of the bed before rearranging himself in a heap
against the fat quilted comforter.

Through the barely opened slits of the shutters,
Franny peered down at the street. It was almost time.
Daylight was beginning to sneak mysteriously round
the corners and up behind the rooftop silhouettes of
the well-tended brownstones and brick apartment
buildings across the way. Gray tinged with streaks
of pink and blue, daylight was just catching up with
the glow of the streetlamps, and West Seventy-fourth
Street looked magical and eerie, as if anything might
happen in the chill of the New York City dawn.

Franny turned from gazing at the empty street to
the large paperback edition of *The Joy of Sex* that lay
open in her lap. Her hand was resting on an illustration of two lovers so strangely entwined that she
guessed they must be Eastern, for only a lifetime of

disciplined meditation and yoga exercises could make the bizarre posture less than excruciatingly painful. Or, for that matter, possible. Still, the lovers were smiling benignly into one another's black outlined eyes. They were probably Persian, she decided, for the illustration was as colorful and complicated as one of her grandmother's precious Persian rugs.

She turned the pages, flipping through a portfolio of lovers in every stage and posture of passion, stopping here and there where a particular drawing captured her attention. The illustrations, however, held less interest for her than the blank pages at the back of the book. On one of these pages were strange notations scrawled in pencil. Dates and times, meticulously recorded. Her finger moved down the list, which began with the printed entry *September 11, 6:15 A.M.* and ended with *October 1, 5:45 A.M.* Her heartbeat quickened, sounding hollow against her chest, and an indigestible lump of fear lodged in her throat. She glanced through the discreetly parted shutters. He was there.

Paul Philips, Franny's father, appeared between two parked cars, looked up and down the empty one-way street, and fidgeted in his pocket for his house keys as he crossed to the handsome brick brownstone in which the Philips family lived. He was dressed for work, almost. Going to or coming from, it was hard to tell because his suits were all so similar. He was wearing one of the regulars—charcoal brown, gray, or blue, it was a toss-up in the early light. But the vest was definitely unbuttoned. His shirt was open at the neck, and his dark tie was neatly folded and tucked into the breast pocket of his jacket. He was carrying an attaché case, too. He looked something like the management consultant he was; something like someone who advised people about how to run their businesses more efficiently. But he also looked, Fran thought, closing the shutters carefully in case he glanced up, like someone who could use a little help getting his own business in order.

His eyes, which had always been deep set, were now sunken in hollows of flesh and bone so deep that they seemed to be begging, in their watery blue way, for someone to rescue them before they disappeared entirely. His hair was slightly windswept, uncovering a bit of naked scalp that Fran had never noticed before, although she supposed it must have been lurking under his straight sandy hair all the time.

Somehow, the forward hunch of his shoulders, the dark hollows around his eyes, and his slightly disheveled appearance all seemed part and parcel with the strange balding spot at the top of his head. And the whole package, this new dawn-creeping creature that was still Paul Philips, her father, seemed part and parcel with changes that were similar to the growing out of—growing up too fast for—one's old pink flannel pajamas.

Franny ran her hand through her hair and hopped down from the window seat. Shag stirred as she padded past the bed. She waited until he'd settled himself again before continuing to her desk where she took a pencil out of the gingham holder, licked it, and turned to the blank pages at the back of *The Joy of Sex. October 2,* she wrote at the bottom of the list, and, glancing at her Mickey Mouse wristwatch just to be certain, she added: 6:00 A.M. Then she closed the book very quietly, as if the cover colliding with the pages would produce a sound to shake the universe. Within five minutes, *The Joy of Sex* was nestled in her bookcase behind Sendak, Milne, E. B. White, and the latest anthology from *Mad* magazine, and Franny Philips had tiptoed back to bed.

Chapter Two

Paul crossed West Seventy-fourth Street and stopped to stare with disgust into the gutter where a delinquent dog walker had neglected to clean up after what appeared to be a (mercifully) constipated Yorkie. Part of Paul's anger was that of a righteous law-abiding citizen; the other part, he realized, feeling his shoulders hunch and shrink in keeping with his own pettiness, was that he'd wished the mess was Shaggylon's and the felon his wife Madeleine. He wished there was something real, something tangible that he could blame her for. But no, not these pathetic little pebbles.

He opened his attaché case, tore a leaf from his yellow legal pad, scooped up the dainty mess, and deposited it into one of the large brown plastic trash cans that stood in front of what was unanimously acknowledged to be the showplace of the block—the Philips town house, with its black lacquered door and brass carriage lamp, its redwood boxes of now fading, chilled geraniums and mums that sat on the ledge of the stoop. Even the little black and red door decal reading These Premises Protected by the Holmes Protective Agency was discreet and tasteful.

He checked to be certain that the carriage lamp was still lighted, then, shaking his head at the absurd importance he placed on that welcoming beacon, he unlocked the door, reached inside, and shut the light.

5

Better, he thought. The warm yellow glow was gone, the gray morning at his back. The grim future was just ahead, up the burnished wooden staircase where Wonder Woman slept like a sack of rocks. His shoes squeaked. His shoes always squeaked these days. They were good leather, supple, but not as lustrously waxed, not as pampered or polished as they used to be. What could she expect, he thought as he squeaked maliciously up the stairs, not that a mere squeak, no matter how malicious, could rouse Madeleine.

He stopped at the head of the stairs. For a moment, he thought he heard Shag growling low in Franny's room. Then the sound diminished to a contained sort of whine—almost as if Fran had deliberately shushed the great shaggy beast. He considered peeking into the room just to have a look at his daughter's sleep-soft face, the little-girl sweetness that giggled awake each morning only to disguise itself in the denim rags of a twelve year old by breakfast time. No, he decided. It was far too early. And if she woke and saw him at this hour, up and dressed, creased and squeaking, she'd want to know why, and he couldn't—absolutely wouldn't—tell her. No matter what Madeleine said.

So he went straight ahead, following the polyurethaned brick wall that led into the master suite and formed a headboard wall behind the king-sized bed in which Madeleine slept. Paul slipped out of his suit jacket and closed the bedroom door behind him. In the thin light, he performed his morning ritual without glancing at his wife or taking pains to be particularly quiet. She was, of course, asleep on her side of the bed. His side, nearest the bathroom, was pristine, undisturbed.

He took his tie from his jacket pocket and hung it on the tie rack in his closet. He checked his jacket, searching the pockets for scraps, paper clips, loose change, lint; then, deciding that it needed pressing, he draped the jacket over the back of a chair. He sat down, took off his shoes, and massaged his feet briefly before reaching under the chair for his shoe trees. He slipped the blond wood shoe trees into the shoes and carried them to the closet. He removed his vest and trousers and, finally, in his unobtrusively pale shirt, white underwear, and dark socks, he went into the bathroom.

Madeleine never stirred.

The digital clock clicked to 6:30 as Paul returned, dressed in striped pajamas. He lifted his corner of the rust and blue printed quilt and climbed into bed. Lost between the bold autumn colors of the matching designer sheets and pillowcases, he closed his eyes and slept. At precisely 6:45, the alarm sounded. He dropped one bare foot then the other onto the floor, clicked open his red-rimmed eyes, and hauled his body to a sitting position. Madeleine slept on undisturbed.

Chapter Three

Franny nestled in her bed. Resting her cheek against Shaggylon's back, she stared at the half inch of space between the bottom of her bedroom door and the top of her rug. She'd heard the alarm go off, heard her father's feet thud to the floor. Now she watched and waited for the silhouette of his ankles to appear in the hall-lit crack beneath her door.

At 6:50, the shadow appeared. She closed her eyes and rolled onto her back a moment before he entered. Shag bounded from the bed to leap and lap at Paul who patted him distractedly. Through the spider-fringed edges of light that came through her eyelids, Franny could make out her father's tall form shuffling to the window to open the shutters. Then he walked over to her bed and stood staring down at her.

She felt the lump in her throat dissolve and liquify, creeping into her nose and eyes, and she fought the stinging sensation with a blink that took in exactly what she thought she'd see if her eyes had been wide open all the time: her father, face melting with some strange sorrow, staring at her, his lost-looking eyes floating blue and helpless with love.

The moment he saw her blink, he smiled. "Okay, Miss Slug-a-Bed, it's time," he chanted, sitting down beside her on the bed.

"Five more minutes," she whispered.

Her voice was deep; not so deep as her mother's,

but getting there. Madeleine had a husky, dusky voice that changed her pretty face into something entirely more substantial; something glamorous. It wasn't like the shrieking, smoking, gravelly voices of women who shouted their beauty away, but a seductive humming sound that underlined simple words and made them seem mysterious. Her own voice, Franny knew, was unusually deep for a kid's, but not yet as consistent or mellow as Madeleine's.

"There are chores to be done, lady." Her father stroked her cheek as he recited the morning litany. "Who's going to water the milk?" he asked, frowning. "Who's going to butter the cream?" He tickled her and she squirmed to a sitting position and threw her arms around his neck. "Who's going to scratch the chickens?" he whispered against her ear.

"Stop," Franny giggled breathlessly.

Paul kissed her. "Okay, pumpkin," he said, holding her at arms' length and studying her face with a distracted solemnity. "On your feet." He turned as if to go, but Franny put her hand on his shoulder.

"Pa?"

He looked at her. His face turned pale, his eyes blindly liquid. She could feel his fear. Tell me, she wanted to say; trust me, daddy. But his face and eyes and even the disheveled look of his sandy hair—under which she now knew there was a secret balding place —all seemed to beg her not to ask, not to urge, not yet.

"What's the capital of Kansas?" she said, and she could see his fear turn to puzzled relief.

"Kansas?"

"Flat Kansas. We're having a geography test."

Paul stroked her arm while he thought about it. Then he sang softly: "Nothing could be feen-er than to be in Ab-il-een-a in the mor-r-r-ning . . ."

"Abilen-a?"

"Wichita," he said decisively. "Brush your teeth."

She waited until he'd left the room before she let the corners of her phony smile droop. "Wichita," she murmured, hauling herself out of bed. "Wichita."

It didn't take her long to dress—about two minutes to scramble out of her pajamas and into a pair of grungy jeans, a wrinkled pink turtleneck, and a plaid shirt which she checked for holes and, finding one at the elbow and a fair-sized rip in the side seam, deemed acceptable. She added sweat socks and a stiffening pair of Adidas sneakers.

"Wichita," she repeated, and she slipped the red shoelace with her house key on it over her head, grabbed her hairbrush, and headed downstairs.

The kitchen was flooded with sunlight that reflected off the deluxe appliances, the hanging copper pots and pans, and the plants. Franny tucked her brush into what was left of the back pocket of her jeans, dialed the wall phone, and, as it started to ring at the other end, took the Minute Maid out of the refrigerator and began to guzzle orange juice straight from the container.

Chapter Four

In the spacious kitchen of the Peterfreund's Central Park West apartment, Barbara was grinding beans. She poured the specially blended Zabar's coffee beans into the little white Braun electric she'd picked up at the duty-free shop in Saint Thomas on her way home from Caneel Bay. Sometimes she thought of the coffee grinder as her dowry. She'd gone to Caneel to forget everything, most of all Ralph and the divorce, and she'd come back feeling terribly attractive. Freckled, pink-tinted, and beginning to peel, but *free*. So free that the beautiful little Braun, the best, they all said, had become a symbol of her independence.

She'd bought it on a whim as an homage to her new found strength. Barbara, the late Mrs. Ralph Harris, didn't need a man to break beans for. No, she was going to drink fresh coffee, ground in the finest machine available, all by her strong new self. But even as she paid for the grinder, she'd been thinking about Simon. She'd been silently thanking Dr. Simon Peterfreund for helping her learn how to buy something excellent and pleasurable just for herself, just because she was worth it!

The little Braun whirred with Teutonic precision, and Barbara, the new Mrs. Dr. Peterfreund, smiled, remembering that Caribbean trip. She glanced over at the table where Jamie sat stuffing natural cereal into his mouth and cartoons from the tiny table Sony into his mind. One canceled out the other, she supposed, fighting the quick stab of guilt. Should she shut off the TV and make him read the *Times* with his breakfast? The helium high voices of Tom and Jerry were almost drowned out by the drone of the Braun. And anyway, he was eating granola. That was healthy, wasn't it? It ought to be, Barbara surmised. Anything that looked like pebbles and tasted like cardboard ought to have some redeeming value.

The water was boiling in the kettle on the stove. The French porcelain drip pot was warm and ready to receive the heavenly smelling coffee. Her son was with her, sharing a lovely new life in a lovely new home with a wonderful *real* man to model himself after. She had everything to be grateful for.

Let him watch cartoons.

Jamie was all that was left of her relationship with the rat. Of course, as Simon pointed out, she'd participated in her own unhappiness, for hadn't she spent years playing mouse to Ralph's rat? Her remorseful heart filled with love for her son. She thanked God for him—and for the fact that he was fair like her. As fair as Ralph was dark. As quiet as Ralph was loud. As good as Ralph was bad.

The telephone's ring ended her exercise in pettiness. Or was it assertiveness? "Hello?" she said.

"Is Jamie there, please?" A child's voice. Pleasant, polite. Barbara was pleased.

"It's for you," she told her son.

"Is that for me?" Simon asked, entering the kitchen. He was freshly showered and shaved, his moustache dashingly attractive, his dark hair properly trimmed —like a grown-up, Barbara thought, remembering how Ralph's hair had reflected his immaturity, his insecurity. Straightened one week, curled the next, blow-dried or butch; a man for all Sassoons, she thought, delighted with the pun and saving it to share with Simon when Jamie was out of earshot.

Simon was in his vest, shirt sleeves, and well-tailored trousers. His jacket was probably on the hanger in his office, which was a two-room suite at the front of the apartment: a waiting room with a sensible sit-up couch, and a "workroom" with a weathered leather analyst's couch, proud victim of tears, sweat, hair stains, squirming backsides, grasping hands, desperate fingernails, and angry heels.

"It's for Jamie," Barbara said, extending the receiver, stretching the flexible wall phone cord to meet her son halfway.

"Hi," he mumbled into the mouthpiece without taking his eyes from the manic high jinks on TV.

Simon kissed her lightly on the forehead. "I'm low on Kleenex," he said, confirming that he'd just come from the office area.

Chapter Five

Jamie sucked a granola flake from his braces and tossed his sandy hair back from his forehead. His face was utterly emotionless, turned (tuned it almost seemed) to the tabletop Sony.

But beneath his high forehead lurked a formidable brain, nurtured on a need for survival in a world ruled by mind-bogglingly irrational adults, yet still hungry for new information, new contests. The most important tool of survival, Jamie had learned, was flexibility, which made it possible to love both his parents without hurting either one. To do this, he'd developed a low profile. Mumbling helped. When one parent ranted about the other, a mumble could be construed as supportive without being provocative or approving. Not understanding adults was another ploy—made manifest by masking all concern with what they did or why they did it or, in extremes, that they did anything at all.

Jamie Harris was an expert. And Franny Philips was achingly new to the game. He could hear the distress in her voice.

"He was right on time," she was saying. "This is the third week. Jamie, I'm going to say something."

"Wrong."

Though he still faced the TV screen, in his peripheral vision he saw his mother opening the Kleenex cabinet—cartons of Kleenex bought for Simon's distraught patients—and the slim, dark shadow of Melody approaching the kitchen. Conflict, his trained brain warned.

"He's made a friend," Barbara whispered happily to Simon.

"I told you. Children are flexible. They adjust."

Jamie's stomach churned with the knowledge that the tender shoot of happiness Franny's telephone call had sown for his mother was about to be plucked by the unhappiest mother-plucker of all: his angry, icy new stepsister, Melody Peterfreund. Just remember that she'll be leaving for college soon, mom, he willed silently. Then he tried, through an even deeper silence, to send a message to Franny at the other end of the phone.

"Good morning, Melody."

He heard the lilting optimism in his mother's voice. There was, of course, no answer. With curdling condescension, Melody's flannel-clad form swept past Barbara. "Good morning, Barbara." Jamie's mother murmured the reply to herself.

Melody lifted the telephone cord with two fingers, as disdainfully as if she were holding the tail of a dead mouse. She slipped under the cord, switched off the cartoons Jamie was watching, and turned to a PBS yoga show in progress.

Jamie held the phone receiver to his ear and said nothing to Melody. What was there to say to someone who obviously enjoyed watching people wrap their toes around their ears or stare into the camera with distended eyeballs and tongues, necks bulging with strained veins? Melody had merely chosen live cartoons over invented ones. No problem. Just that the lullaby level of the music accompanying the yoga exercises was less hospitable to his privacy than the slam-bam frenzy of Tom and Jerry.

"Ja-mie—" Franny's funny deep voice urged.

He stared at the TV silently.

"I'm making coffee," Barbara told Melody. Without a word, the girl walked to the cabinet and took out a jar of instant Maxwell House. Barbara turned helplessly to Simon who glanced at the kitchen clock.

"Hirschfield's late," he said.

"How can he pay for an hour of your time and always be late?"

"If he knew, he wouldn't be here—"

Jamie caught the non sequitur and tried not to put it in its place, which was in the minus column of the ledger he'd recently opened—against his better judgment—on Simon. In general, Jamie was strictly laissez-faire when it came to his parents' mating choices. They were simply beyond comprehension. But since he'd found himself grading his father's ever-changing procession of girl friends, he felt it at least fair to apply the same standard to his mother's new mate. In general, Simon was doing okay.

"You can't talk," Franny said at last.

"Right." The faintest smile crossed his lips, caught on his braces, and disappeared before anyone in the Peterfreund kitchen could notice it.

"You still want me to go tomorrow?"

"Sure."

"Okay." She sounded slightly reassured. "I'll ask my mom. She's asleep, so it's the best time to ask her." When he didn't respond, her apprehension returned and crackled through the wires in a single word: "Jamie?"

"See ya," he said and hung up.

Melody cruised past him, her cup of coffee in her hand. She was tall and dark-haired and had a brittle spinsterly air that superseded reality. Reality was that Melody was only eighteen and probably mushy. Jamie had the definite impression that if she dared relax her wire-tight shoulders or move with anything less than mannequin precision, she'd probably wind up in a sloppy heap at Simon's feet. Who else but a scared cream puff would go up against his tiny, fragile mother constantly armored for combat?

To make things worse, her father was a shrink, a professional psychiatrist whose *job* it was to understand and help perfect strangers. If Simon understood Melody—if she *let* him understand and help her— she'd probably feel like a perfect stranger to him. So there she was, stuck; a cream puff iced with anger.

Simon touched Melody's arm. "Are you going to school today?" She kept on walking and he followed her. "Melody," he said as if he were talking to Mr. Hirschfield, "I'd like you to go to school today."

The doorbell rang and Simon went to answer it.

"Who was that?" Barbara asked Jamie.

"Probably Mr. Hirschfield."

"On the phone."

"Just a kid," he said. He switched the channel back to his cartoons and sat down with the granola again.

"I'm glad you're making friends," his mother said. She started out using her new assertive voice, but then it slipped back to the cozy warm place it used to come from. "I know it's hard. A new school. A new family—"

Tom went stalking out of the frame on two legs with his paws swinging aggressively. Jerry, also on two feet, scampered after him apologetically. It looked, just a little, like Simon following Melody out of the kitchen. Jamie laughed.

Barbara ran her fingers through his hair. "I just want you to know," she said, "that I think you're adjusting beautifully, Jamie."

Chapter Six

Franny ran up the stairs into her parents' room. The bathroom door was closed, but she could hear her father's electric razor starting up. She moved quickly over to the bed where Madeleine slept. "Ma," she whispered loudly, "ma, you've got to make my braid." She pulled the brush out of her back pocket and glanced apprehensively at the bathroom door again. Paul hadn't heard her. Neither had Madeleine.

Franny shook her mother gently.

"Yes. What? Right," Madeleine rasped, and she hauled herself, eyes shut, thick hair frazzled with static cling, to something resembling a sitting position, blue denim nightshirt up against the wall, head listing toward the comforter.

"Ma?"

Madeleine held her hand up. Without lifting her head, she reached toward the night table and her fingers closed skillfully around her cigarette pack. She tossed her head back slowly, let her sleep-puffed lids roll up, and stared with glazed eyes first at her daughter and then at her cigarettes. Franny thrust the hairbrush into her hand before she had time to choose, and Madeleine smiled graciously, relinquishing the cigarettes.

"Don't hurt but make it tight."

Madeleine slid her feet out from under the quilt,

18

placed them firmly on the floor, and, perched at the edge of her bed, started brushing.

"You're hurting," Franny said.

"I'm not hurting," Madeleine replied hoarsely.

"It's *my* head."

"Hold still."

Fran, her back toward Madeleine, smiled. Even with her mother's deep morning voice, the distance between them was diminishing octave by octave.

"Can I have a sleep-over tomorrow? It's Friday."

Madeleine grunted. Franny put up her arm. There was a ponytail holder around her wrist. Madeleine removed it and fastened it around the end of the braid she'd accomplished by braille or the radar that guided her through the first ten minutes of wakening.

"Can I?"

"Here?"

"At Jamie's," Franny said evenly.

Madeleine grunted again and, squinting at her handiwork, fell back against the pillows. She lifted an arm to stroke her daughter's dewy face, missed by a good six inches, and let her hand flutter down to rest. She was almost asleep by the time it landed. Franny leaned over and kissed her on the forehead. "Thanks, ma," she said, "that's neat."

"Brush your teeth," said Madeleine. But Franny was gone. Madeleine blinked, sighed, thought twice, then stood up and made her way to the bathroom.

Paul, in his pajama bottoms, was leaning over one of two oval basins examining his freshly shaved face in the mirror. Madeleine glided past him deftly on her way to the toilet. He emptied the bristles from his electric razor into the basin and turned to put on the shower. Madeleine washed her hands on her side, the window side, of the sink and plucked a tissue from the box. She balled up the Kleenex in her fingers and, on her way out of the room, wiped the shaving bristles from Paul's basin.

"Had to do it, didn't you?" he hissed at her as if she were a kinky kleptomaniac caught once again pocketing his chin hairs on the sly.

She jerked her thumb in the direction of the steaming stall. Still half asleep, she growled, "Shower, Paul."

"I showered," he shouted. Then, glancing furtively into the bedroom, he looked both ways and continued in a lower voice. "I showered before I got here. I shave here. And then I shower again. I shower again because Franny knows I shower after I shave. Only now I shower there and then I shave and shower here and let me tell you—"

Madeleine went back into the bedroom. Paul followed her. "What do you care—" He let his recitation trail off.

She walked around to her side of the bed and took a cigarette.

"I don't care what you say," he said to the pale blue fumes of her smoke. "We are not going to inflict our problems on an innocent child. That's the way it is."

Madeleine tucked her short nightshirt under her, sat down on the bed, and stood up again, instantly stung. She pulled Franny's hairbrush out from under her bare thigh and muttered, "Nuts!"

"Don't give me that 'I've heard it before and I don't want to hear it again' stuff." Paul was selecting underwear from the built-in dresser. He was half hidden behind the louvered closet door. "Franny is not going to be another unwanted, neurotic victim of irresponsible divorced parents."

Madeleine thumped the back of the brush against her palm, weighing it, considering her chances of hitting him at such a distance. She set the hairbrush down in her lap. Only a boomerang would make it round the closet door.

"You think it's fun to put on your socks twice every morning?" he asked. "You think it's a joy—up at five, shower, race here and wake her up and make jokes, and then shave and shower again? By one o'clock I'm a zombie, and what do you care? You just lie there unconscious."

Madeleine let the hairbrush slide to the floor, took a long drag on her cigarette, and laid back down in bed. "Paul—"

"I don't care," he announced, shaking a pair of fresh socks at her. "She's worth it. That's it. The bottom line. And when I'm ready, that's when we'll tell her that her mother and father are a disaster area. So right now, don't hock at me, hear?" And he marched back into the bathroom, slammed the door, opened it again immediately, and, in a perfectly ordinary, even polite, voice, said, "That suit's got to go to the cleaners."

Chapter Seven

Shag was squatting in the street just half a block from the West Side School, a progressive private school housed in a structure that looked a little like a building and a lot like a giant television set. It was tall for a TV, but shorter by several stories than the towering prewar apartment houses that flanked it along West End Avenue. Prefab concrete and picture-tube glass, ovaled oddly, the school looked—even if its students didn't—affluent.

There was something surreal, Paul thought, about a school that was shaped like a television set and appeared, each morning, to be swallowing the cast of *Oliver*—a procession of ragamuffins disgorged from sleek limousines, yellow cabs, private school buses, and the firm grasps of an army of multicolored nursemaids. From four years old to thirteen, male or female, the students of the West Side School dressed in the universal uniform of most $3000-a-year progressive New York private schools: jeans, sneakers, windbreakers; radical tatters.

Paul held Shag's leash and watched the strange building ingesting its performers. Franny, eyes fixed pessimistically on Shag's haunches, held the pooper-scooper—a small plastic bag opened like a butterfly net at the end of a specially designed stick.

"If he doesn't do it, dad, I'm going to be late."

"Shag," Paul said, "has needs, too."

"Oh daddy," she sighed with frustration. "Four late slips and I get an after-school!"

"I'll write an excuse."

"Oh, great. 'Dear Mrs. Hackett, Franny is late today because her dog can't take a sh—'"

"Franny!"

She hunched her shoulders, half apologetic, half defiant.

"Just because your mother has a mouth like a teamster—"

"She does not!"

It was as if she'd slapped him. His eyes went all soft and watery again and the hollows beneath them seemed to darken as an embarrassed flush crept up from his cheeks. Then he looked over her head to the tops of the autumn trees at the edge of Riverside Park. "I didn't say that word until I was eighteen," he told the trees, "and nobody thought I was retarded."

"M'sorry," Franny murmered. "Honest." He shrugged, and when he continued staring off into space, she turned toward the park, too, just in time to see Jamie Harris approaching. He'd apparently just gotten off the bus and was walking toward the school with a number of other kids. His clothes set him apart immediately: navy blue prep school blazer, buttondown shirt, gray flannel pants, and real shoes. And he had a book bag, not an army-navy surplus knapsack, slung over his thin shoulders.

Franny began to smile, but Jamie's grim face urged her to be cautiously casual. She could see him giving Paul the once-over, fast but thorough. And then he was abreast of them, nodding curtly to her.

"Hi," she said.

"Hi," he mumbled.

"Who was that?" Paul asked, looking after the immaculately groomed, remarkably somber boy.

"He's new," Franny said.

"Do they let him in, dressed like a human being?"

"He can't help it," she said. "He had to wear that in his last school and his mother won't buy him new jeans."

"Why not?"

"His father won't give her the money."

"For jeans?" Paul said incredulously.

"They're split and they're having a fight about charge accounts."

His eyes shot open and his jaw dropped in honest outrage. "You mean—" He shook his head, appalled. "Because of their problems, the poor kid has to go to school like—like a freak?"

"You just said he looked like a human being."

"You'd better hurry," Paul decided. "You don't want to get a late slip." He kissed her on the forehead, tenderly, but quickly enough not to embarrass her; then he took the pooper-scooper from her hand.

She turned to say good-bye to Shag who was just shaking his rear end in a grand finale of relief and pride. "Good boy," she called to him, then waved once more to Paul and ran up the street to disappear in the tangle of faded denim storming the school.

Jamie was waiting for her on the second-floor landing. She saw him leaning against the wall, reading a paperback, while the horde swirled around him. Five year olds scampered like spider monkeys among preteens cocooned in baby fat, tall skinny rubber-limbed boys and girls with hair frizzed and flying, early skiers already on crutches, and late Hamptons and Fire Island weekenders snuffling beach colds into pocket-sized Kleenex—all milling, shouting, whirling, shlepping. The din was deafening.

"Can you go?" Jamie shouted as they climbed the stairs together.

"Yup."

"Neat."

"Well," Franny said, "you saw him."

Jamie nodded gravely. "It's all there."

"You're sure?"

"It figures," he said abstractly.

"But you're not sure."

"He's got the look, all right."

She stared at him skeptically. "But how do you know?"

They moved into the corridor together. "You've got to prove it out," he explained. "Like algebra. You've got to find the unknown quotient."

"X equals—" Franny began.

"The other woman. What else?"

She screwed up her face and squinted at him.

"Well, he's not sleeping home—and he's not gay, is he?"

"No," she said defensively.

"Well then—"

They were at Mrs. Hackett's classroom. "Oooohhh," Franny moaned. "I've got a geography test and now I can't remember anything except the capital of Kansas!"

"Topeka."

"No. Wichita."

"Topeka," Jamie said with quiet arrogance.

"No!" she gasped.

"Topeka."

"But he told me Wichita!"

"That proves it."

"What?"

"The equation," he explained patiently. "When there's another woman on their mind, they screw everything up."

Franny entered the classroom. "Topeka. Darn," she mumbled. "Topeka!"

Chapter Eight

After geography, the sixth-grade, two classrooms of them including Jamie and Franny, prepared for phys. ed. which, at the West Side School, meant putting on their windbreakers and heading over to the park. Miss Cohen was in charge of the sexually progressive, which meant sexually mixed, teams. Girls and boys together, hard-core softball with no chauvinistic separatism, which was a crock, Franny thought, since most of the sixth-grade boys were scrawnier, shorter, and less coordinated than the girls.

Miss Cohen was young, and she might have been attractive if she weren't always ringing her hands or blowing her whistle. She was pretty tense and it showed up in eccentric mannerisms, sudden shudders and odd voice changes, and unnecessary shouting that began on an admonitory note and ended often in little high-pitched yelps and ineffectual, vague summary sentences. She brought her whistle to her lips now to call for a straightening of the undisciplined line of students preparing to cross to the park. Miss Cohen did things like that. She put store in the intrinsic goodness of standing straight in a straight line. In that sense, she was untraditional, at least for the West Side School.

She blew her whistle and readjusted the string bag of softballs and the canvas bag of bats in her charge.

"Okay, now, listen. *Everybody!*" she shrieked. "No talking!"

A fire engine roared by, drowning out the groans and expressions of contempt and disbelief that such a demand, such a wild off-the-wall expectation, justified.

"Quiet!" she continued in the wake of the fire engine. "Now line up. No talking and wait at the light."

Susan Metzger who, in Franny's estimation, was the incumbent candidate for class wimp, sidled up to Miss Cohen. Snuffling to draw attention to her red and runny nose, she thrust a folded sheet of lavender stationery at the nervous phys. ed. teacher. "I've got an excuse and a cold, Miss Cohen. Can I wait at the nurse?"

"Miss Cohen," Franny said, tugging at the arm carrying the string softball bag. "Can I be excused? I've got cramps." She was in no mood for softball. In fact, she was in no mood for anything except trying to figure out the X quotient, and Susan Metzger's cold had provided on-the-spot inspiration for getting out of the boring ball game.

"Jonathan, back!" Miss Cohen shrilled at a short, squirmy boy who had one leg in the gutter. "What?" she said to Franny.

"You know. Cramps."

Miss Cohen tucked the lavender letter into her pocket without reading it. She glanced distractedly at the waiting girls. "You can both come and watch," she decided. "The air'll do you good. It's a beautiful day." And as she turned back to the street a passing bus discharged a raspberry of rank fumes. Miss Cohen coughed, sneezed, and sputtered.

Franny and Susan walked to the back of the line, and Jamie smiled noncommittally as Franny passed.

The right side of his upper lip stuck for a moment on a treacherous section of his braces and, as he ran his tongue along his gum to free it, he was relieved that Franny seemed too preoccupied to have noticed either the smile or the lopsided lip. He was not pleased, however, about how disturbed she seemed. She was altogether too transparent for her own good. Susan, with all her wimpy wheezing and snuffling, looked far healthier, and that was definitely uncool. Also, Susan *had* noticed his lip and had snickered.

"I'll sit with you," Susan told Franny.

"I don't want your cold."

"I'm not catching anymore. My mother said."

"I want *quiet* in this line!" Miss Cohen shouted. Then the light changed and she blew her whistle. "Okay. Let's move!"

"Have you really got it?" Susan whispered when she and Franny were settled in, side by side, on a bench several yards from the two teams.

"Got what?" Franny blinked herself back from the confusion of her thoughts.

Susan looked over her shoulder into the bushes behind the bench and, seeing no one lurking near, continued in her conspiratorial whisper, "You know—"

"Say it," Franny demanded.

"*You* know."

"My period," Franny said with vicious indifference.

Susan flushed and shuddered. "I know I'm going to get it at school," she whispered breathlessly. She snuffled and wiped her nose on the sleeve of her L.L. Bean down parka. "I'm going to get up to answer a question," she continued tremulously. "I'm going to go to the board to answer a question and it's going to be running down my leg."

"I don't have it," Franny said dully.

"But you said—"

"I don't want to play stupid softball. Shut up, Susan."

"But—"

Franny pinned the quivering girl with as icy a look as she could manage. "I've got to think," she announced by way of apology.

It wasn't another woman, she was almost sure of that. Her dad wasn't the type . . . but then, what did she know about the type anyway—any type? She tried to imagine Paul with his eyes painted, outlined in black, wearing slick sideburns and a Persian moustache. No way. There wasn't a single illustration in the whole book that she could picture him a part of.

"Leslie can't even hit," Susan said.

Franny didn't answer. She was leafing through the book in her mind, trying—just to be fair—to imagine Madeleine as a participant in *The Joy of Sex*. There was one very loving, not terribly exciting, picture of a couple in which the woman, partially dressed and viewed from the back, had thick hair something like her mother's and nice legs, although at first glance it'd been hard to tell which of the four intertwining legs was whose.

"I think Jamie Harris is a nerd."

Because of her cold, it sounded as though Susan Metzger thought Jamie Harris was a turd—which would have been, in keeping with developing a more colorful vocabulary, a definite step up for the wimp. Franny glanced at her with mild interest before she realized that it was only a stuffed nose that had inadvertently lifted Susan out of the personality pit in which she normally languished. She shook her head and resumed her contemplation.

Unless something dire occurred between now and about six tomorrow evening, she would be spending Friday night with Jamie and his father, Ralph. It was a plan with a two-part purpose. Jamie believed the experience would offer her a pragmatic preview of one of the realities of life in a divided family. Also, if anyone knew anything about infidelity—or the X quotient—it was Ralph. He was, Jamie'd claimed between math period and the geography test this morning, the man who put the X in eXpert on that topic. And there was absolutely nothing you couldn't talk frankly about with Ralph.

Jamie, however, had cautioned Fran that he himself rarely asked his father anything. He didn't have to. His father shared just about everything with him. Well, Jamie had amended with rare shyness, everything short of *everything*, of course. But if Franny had any questions about her own father's odd new behavior, Ralph had impeccable credentials and more than enough practical experience to offer at least an educated guess.

The second reason for spending the night together was simpler. Where and when else would they ever find the time and the privacy to discuss Franny's family situation as fully and seriously as it seemed to warrant. Ralph had already mentioned to Jamie that he was bringing along a date; a model or actress or stewardess he'd just met. That, Jamie told Franny, was as good as a written guarantee that the two of them could have as much undisturbed time together as they wanted.

"It's so *boring!*" Susan Metzger whined.

Franny shook her head helplessly. "How can I think if you won't shut up? Phooey," she whispered under her breath. "Here comes Cohen."

Miss Cohen strode toward the bench where the girls were sitting. "I need some base umpires. Susan, you take first and Franny, you take—" The teacher stopped abruptly. That is, her voice stopped. Her mouth continued to move, silently, convulsively, for a second or two as her eyes widened with disbelief. She was looking beyond the bench into the low brambles behind it. "Oh, no," she gasped at last.

Franny turned to follow Miss Cohen's wide-eyed gaze, but the young teacher stepped forward, grabbed both girls, and inexplicably crushed their faces against her chest. "Don't look!" she ordered. Then, addressing the bushes behind them, she shrieked, "Go away! Get out of here, you pervert!"

"I can't breathe," Susan mumbled into Miss Cohen's sweat shirt.

"Police! Where are the police?"

The gym teacher's whistle was etching its outline into Franny's forehead, and with a fierce effort Franny broke free of Miss Cohen's grip and managed to peer round at the brambles. A small, frightened man in a quiet business suit and a simple pale hat was standing, half hidden by the bushes. His conservative belt was unbuckled and his pants were open—wide open!

"Don't look, Franny!" Miss Cohen shouted. "Don't turn around. Police!" She grabbed her whistle and blew it.

The shrill sound nearly deafened the girls, and the scared little man hobbled and ran deeper into the bushes, tripping over his trouser cuffs. The first recognizable sound Franny heard, once the shrill of the whistle cleared her ears, was the unmistakable *zzzzit* of his zipper closing.

The children on the softball field, assuming that the whistle signaled the end of the physical education period, began gathering their windbreakers, softballs, and bats, and started drifting toward the bench. Miss Cohen, whose face was hidden in her hands, didn't see them coming.

"All I want to do is my job!" she sobbed. "I want healthy bodies for healthy minds! I want fitness, and I get perverts and rapists and muggers in the morning with the sun shining and—" She threw back her head. *"Police!"* she screamed. "I can't stand it anymore! I can't bear it! *Help!* Nobody helps. Nobody cares!"

"It's all right, Miss Cohen." Franny tried to reassure the hysterical teacher.

"It's *not* all right! It's never going to be all right! Children! We're going back! Form a line! Back! *Where are the police?*" she bellowed wildly. "We'll do sit-ups! We'll do jumping jacks! I'm not coming into this park again. I will not come into this park again—"

Franny began to stroke Miss Cohen's back. "Honest, it's okay, Miss Cohen. He's gone. He didn't hurt us."

"Who?" Susan asked, glancing guiltily at the wet spot her squashed nose had left on Miss Cohen's sweat shirt.

Franny ignored her. "We're all here," she told the teacher in a voice as soothing as her stroking hand, "and we'll all line up and we'll go back."

"I missed it," Susan complained to Jamie and Elliot who, along with some of the other students, were assembling near the bench. "Why do I miss everything?"

"Blow your whistle, Miss Cohen," Franny said softly. "It's okay. Honest."

Tears streaming down her face, Miss Cohen blew the whistle. The curious but tolerant sixth graders led her gingerly from the park.

Chapter Nine

By three o'clock, most of the upper school knew about Miss Cohen's encounter with the flasher. Susan Metzger, holding court on the low wall surrounding the squat ovaled building, answered questions about the incident in a voice that vacillated between the dry factuality of Betty Furness and the wet fervor of Rona Barrett. Jamie and Franny decided to leave school separately, five minutes apart, Franny walking north and Jamie south, and to double back and meet some blocks away at the frozen yogurt store on Broadway.

Jamie ordered a scoop of natural honey with carob sprinkles. Franny opted for vanilla.

"Why can't I just ask him where he goes to sleep every night?" she said as they walked toward her house.

"Except weekends," Jamie reminded her, turning his cone deftly, circling the overflow of honey-flavored yogurt with his tongue. "Weekends he sleeps home because you're home."

"Why can't I? Why can't I say it? Why can't I just ask Where do you go every night, pa? Where do you sleep?"

"Because," he replied patiently, "they don't want you to know."

Franny glared at him, then took a solid, achingly cold bite of her yogurt. Her dark brows lowered sul-

33

lenly. Her deep blue eyes, Paul's eyes everyone said,
flinched, as much from frustration as from the sudden chill of the frozen cone. She licked at the yogurt
viciously, paring it down as if it were the problem—
a problem one could lick, so to speak, or at least
reduce to a size one could swallow. "Phooey," she
muttered.

Jamie raised his feathery brown eyebrows.

"Boy," Franny said, sighing. "They spend three
grand to send us to a school where they make such
a big deal about telling the truth—"

"That's school," Jamie reminded her. School and
life, he seemed to be implying, had different les-
sons to teach. After a moment's consideration, she
nodded in understanding. Then she worked dili-
gently and silently on her cone, glancing sideways
at Jamie Harris who, in his methodical way, was doing the same.

Franny studied his sandy hair which was very
straight and medium long and always neat. She noticed a hint of cheekbone hiding under the round,
downy skin that stretched forward as his tongue
reached for the sugar cone. And the late-afternoon
light picked up the fairest trace of pale silky hair on
Jamie's upper lip and just a tickle's worth along his
cheeks. He was shorter than she was, of course
(which of the boys in her class, except that glandular
condition, Jason Lovett, wasn't?), but only by about
an inch. And Jamie was, well, *frail* was and wasn't
the right word.

In some ways, his shoulders, for instance, which were
pretty thin and tended to fold forward, and his wrists,
which were always hanging an inch or so too far out
of his cuffs, he looked frail. But there was just as
much about him that seemed strong, Franny thought
with an odd warmth flooding her face and belly at

the same time. Yes, Jamie Harris was strong in a special way. Strong like in smart. She could imagine his brain as a giant stretching creature—The Hulk, maybe—a tough mass that rippled slowly and worked something like Arnold Shwartzenegger's arms in *Pumping Iron*, slowly, deliberately, with crushing intensity and total confidence.

There was also something strong, she thought, about a boy brand new to a school full of pampered monsters. Franny had overheard a couple of teachers call them that and, though it made her sore and she'd scowled at them in the hall, she thought, after a while, that maybe they were right . . . in a way. Anyhow, here was this new kid dressed like something out of a "Wonderful World of Disney" rerun, like a Mouseketeer left over from TV's black-and-white days or one of Robert Young's kids before he turned into Marcus Welby. Here was this squeaky clean, frail-shouldered boy, with a mouthful of rubber bands and steel, thrust into the pampered monsters' pit—and *he* was helping *her!*

First he'd helped her during study group when the class broke up into four or five kids per table working on similar problems. He'd just looked over at her math folder and asked if she wanted to learn a real easy way to multiply any number by eleven. You just added the two outside numbers and put the sum of them in the middle. Like if you wanted to multiply 12 by 11, you added the 1 and the 2 of 12, came up with 3, and slipped that in the middle: 132! It worked up to about 19, then it got more complicated.

After that, he seemed, well, always available. Not pushing or pulling, just sort of there. And little by little—especially since Myra Michaelson had moved to California with her mother after her parents

split up, and Jennifer Sprawn had transferred to Per-
forming Arts—it had felt all right to hang out with
a boy. Not that they were best friends or anything.
It was just that, in some ways, they were in the same
boat. Her two best friends had left the West Side
School and Jamie was new and without best friends,
too. So they were just helping each other out really.
Just temporarily, until . . .

Franny felt a sudden rush of gratitude toward
Jamie Harris. No one, not Myra or Jennifer, much
as they might have wanted to, could have helped
her, guided her, puzzled through this weird situation with her without spilling the beans. Jamie was—
in the words of Paul Simon—a rock and an island.
And, she thought, almost reaching out to stroke the
sunlit fuzz on his cheek, he really was kind of neat-
looking, too.

"This is it," Franny announced, waving at the black
lacquered door to the brownstone.

"You sure she's out?"

"My ma? Sure. She works for the city. Department of Consumer Affairs. She's real good at it, too.
Takes it seriously I mean. She'd never be home this
early."

"And him?"

"Oh, puh-lease, Jamie. He's a management consultant. He's got to . . . consult, you know. I mean
how could they afford this place if they knocked off
work in the middle of the afternoon? Corine'll be
home, though. But she's neat."

"Corine?"

Franny unlocked the front door with the key that
hung on the shoelace around her neck. "Corine
Johnson, our housekeeper. She's cool—as long as
Shag doesn't shed in her laundry basket."

They walked through the front hall to the remodeled country-style kitchen at the rear of the brownstone.

"Isn't he house-trained yet?" Jamie asked.

"*Shed*—I said 'shed' in the laundry basket."

"Oh," he replied mildly. His impassive eyes studied the weathered patterns of the barn siding and the copper-bottomed pans and well-oiled wok hanging over the butcher block counter across the way. Franny had dumped her knapsack onto the round kitchen table and was already ferreting in a refrigerator that was stocked to outlast a nuclear holocaust.

"There's never anything to eat in this house," she complained.

The door to the basement opened, and Corine, carrying an armful of freshly ironed linens, entered the kitchen. "There's frozen yogurt in the freezer," she told Franny.

"Hi, Corine."

As the housekeeper, who was tall, elegant, and brown, had ascended one set of stairs, Shag, who was squat, gray, and shimmying with undisciplined pleasure, descended the other. Corine moved the clean linen out of harm's way as the beast bounded toward Franny. He greeted her by skidding across the handsomely waxed floor and panting, pink-tongued, tail wagging ecstatically, to a thudding stop.

Franny, with her back to the opened refrigerator and a can of Coke in the hand behind her, rubbed Shag's head.

"Your mother said no Coke weekdays," Corine reminded her, though how she could see behind someone's back was one of the impenetrable mysteries of the household.

Franny put back the Coke. "This is Jamie. He's new."

"How do you do?" Jamie said.

Corine's eyebrows raised at the unexpected politeness. "Considering the stairs," she said with a soft approving smile. "I'm doing fine, thank you." Then she continued across the room and through the swinging door.

Franny pulled a jar of dill pickles out of the refrigerator. She unscrewed the top, dipped her fingers into the brine, and selected a medium-sized pickle for Jamie. "What if—" she began, offering him the dripping dill.

Jamie stopped her. He held up his hand. Head turned toward the door, he waited. When he was sure Corine was out of earshot, he took a fresh pickle from the jar. Franny had already bitten into the first offering.

"What if," she continued, "we go to his office and follow him?"

Jamie wasn't even looking at her. He was walking around inspecting the kitchen. Fran followed him, waiting.

"Say he comes out of his building," Jamie said, still pacing. "Say he doesn't see us. And then say he takes a cab. Then what do we do?" He stopped at the counter-top TV and switched it on. A game show was in progress and Jamie watched it.

"You've got a bus pass," Franny said.

"Right. I jump on a bus. I show the driver my bus pass and I say, 'Follow that cab!' "

Franny reached forward to shut off the TV, but Jamie was circling the kitchen again. "It's just a focusing device I'm experimenting with," he said. "The TV—just a focusing device—like why babies suck their thumbs. You know, their minds are so full of input—color, sound, movement—it's all mixed up because they're not organized yet. Anyway, they've been doing studies on it and they think that thumb-sucking, for babies, serves some sort of neurological purpose; helps to organize the brain so it can concentrate on one thing at a time—or several things, but all in their place—"

He'd reached the kitchen desk. Franny left the television set on. She shook her head in wonder and returned to the refrigerator for an apple.

Behind the handsome little distressed-wood desk, there was a pegboard, and on that pegboard a list of Important Numbers was posted. Jamie's eyes swept the list lazily, top to bottom, and continued down to examine the organized clutter on the desk top: a fabric-covered pencil holder; a doodle pad, blank but for the white imprint of two words—*Brillo* and *Sweet 'n Low;* a sheaf of envelopes stuck in an antique brass toast holder; a letter opener that appeared to be made of ivory but turned out to be plastic; and a telephone book—a bulky address book covered in the same fabric as the pencil holder and dripping business cards and scraps of paper from between its organized A to Z pages.

He picked up the book carefully. Somewhere behind him Franny was murmuring, "They can do anything they want, can't they?" He heard Shag's toenails click over to the back door and begin to paw at it. "They can tell us anything," Franny went on. Then there was the snapping sound of the door lock, a quick chill across the kitchen, and Franny and Shag were out in the garden, where her unhappy monologue continued, floating back to him in disjointed phrases, irate and despairing.

"They can tell us anything. Or not tell us anything. And *we* can't say or do anything. We haven't got one single lousy human right!"

Jamie took the address book out to the garden. Unnoticed, he watched Franny pacing, pleading her

case to the browning geraniums. Her eyes were far
more sad than angry. Her soft husky voice quavered
with helpless indignation. He knew what she was going through. Hadn't he gone through the same thing
when he was a kid?

That was how he thought of it—BD and AD—
Before the Divorce and After the Divorce. BD he'd
been a kid—like her. Not exactly like her, of course,
but then he was a thinker. Franny was a doer and,
worse, a feeler. He had never let them see or know
or even guess what he was feeling, or even whether
he was feeling anything. He'd known what was happening, too. Early on he'd known they were going
to split up, but he hadn't done a thing to interfere
or try to stop it.

Jamie swallowed hard. There was a glob in his throat
and that weird invisible fist in his gut, like there used
to be when he listened to Ralph and Barbara fighting. That's what Franny was doing now—fighting.
And just like his parents, she was bound to lose.
She was too angry, too upset, too wide open. She
was going to get hurt if she wasn't careful.

He swallowed hard. He couldn't have stopped it anyway. There wasn't really anything he could have
done. He knew that absolutely. They'd both told
him that there was nothing *anyone* could do to keep
them together. But why hadn't he tried?

"What United States Constitution?" Franny ranted.

Jamie rubbed the aching empty place where the
invisible fist had struck. "His number is 743-4561 and
he sleeps at 200 West Sixty-ninth Street," he said
suddenly.

"What?"

"His name's Paul, isn't it?" There was a penciled
notation on the inside cover of the address book. He

showed it to her. "Your mom's got to know in case of emergency."

"Jamie," she whispered with unexpected restraint, "you're a genius."

He closed the book and started back to the house. "My IQ's 145. But it's not genius."

Shag followed them inside and stayed so stubbornly near them that there was nothing to do but put on his lead and take him along. They came to that conclusion mutually and without discussion. The idea to go immediately to 200 West Sixty-ninth Street was Franny's. Jamie wasn't crazy about it, but after trying some halfhearted dissuasion, he capitulated.

╫╫

Chapter Ten

They were walking west on Seventy-fourth Street. Jamie was checking the house numbers, trying to estimate which blocks Paul might live between. "I guess it'd be across Columbus." He turned. Franny had stopped a few feet back and was waiting while Shag circled a fire hydrant.

"My father trained him," she explained. "His full name is Master of Shaggylon the Second. My first Shaggylon died. I named them."

"Shaggylon?"

She shrugged. "It's dumb. I made it up. When I was little. This place—Shaggylon—where everything's, you know, perfect. And nobody argues. Or lies." She smiled and shrugged again.

Noticing what nice teeth she had, he ran his tongue over his own, snagging his braces.

"I told you it's dumb," she said. "Anyway—" She tugged at the dog's lead. "Shag doesn't lie. He just pees."

A passing cab slowed down and a frighteningly familiar throaty voice called from the window, "Franny—"

"Oh my God, it's my mom," she said, closing her eyes.

"Hey, it's okay," Jamie whispered. "Relax, will you? We're walking the dog."

"We're walking the dog." She opened her eyes. "Why didn't I think of that?"

They turned together and walked back to the house. Madeleine's cab had stopped in front of it. "You're walking the dog," she said as she climbed out. She sounded surprised and pleased. "Loving a dog is one thing; walking it is another."

"You're early."

"I know. I had a meeting that was canceled." She dragged her attaché case and two large Blooming-dale's shopping bags out of the cab, and she laughed. "So instead of counseling consumers, I consumed."

Jamie glanced at Franny, then nodded impercep-tibly at the shopping bags. There was something about them he seemed to find significant. Did it have to do with the charge account battle that was still raging between his divorced parents? she wondered. Or were wives whose husbands had X quotients stashed away given to sudden midafternoon spend-ing sprees at Bloomingdale's"?

"How are you, Bubbs?" Madeleine asked, kissing Franny.

"This is Jamie."

He held his hand out to her. "How do you do, Mrs. Philips?"

Franny saw the quick confusion cross her mother's face. Momentarily taken aback by Jamie's politeness, she put down a shopping bag to shake his hand. "How do you do, Jamie?"

"He's new," Franny said, explaining his lapse from conventional rudeness.

"I can tell," said Madeleine as Jamie picked up the bags and carried them toward the house.

"Is daddy coming home for dinner?"

Jamie gave her an admonitory look. Her feelings

were too close to the surface again. When was she
going to learn that life wasn't all show-and-tell?

"Of course," Madeleine said coolly, "he'll be home
for dinner."

Franny smiled. If she'd been Shag, her tail would
have been waving, too, Jamie thought. It was that
kind of smile.

"But," Madeleine continued, "I've got to speak at a
senior citizen center."

Franny's elation faded as quickly and obviously
as it had come. Even Madeleine noticed.

"It's important, Franny. There are these generic
drugs, and if they understand that their doctors can
prescribe them, they can save a fortune—"

Franny didn't respond, wouldn't smile, couldn't care
less.

"Franny," Madeleine said softly, "it's my job. I won't
be late. They go to bed early."

"So do I."

There was nothing to do but register the guilt and
change the subject. Madeleine tried. "How was
school?"

"Fine."

"Good."

They'd reached the door. "I've got to go," Jamie
said.

"Why?"

"If I'm not home by five, my mom panics."

Madeleine nodded in sympathetic understanding.
"When you're new, the city can be scary. How long
has she lived here?"

"All her life," Jamie said. Then to Franny, "Six-
thirty. Tomorrow."

Madeleine burrowed in her purse, searching for her
key. "It's nice to meet you, Jamie."

"See you," he said.

"I'll be all packed," Franny called after him.

Madeleine slipped the key into the lock. "That's a nice boy." She smiled approvingly at her daughter. "Packed for what?"

"The sleep-over."

"What sleep-over?"

"I told you. Tomorrow night. At Jamie's."

The key remained unturned. "Hold it—" said Madeleine.

"You said yes."

"Yes to what, when?"

"This morning."

Very slowly, one hand still on the unturned key and the other gripping the shopping bag handles, Madeleine said softly, "Jamie is a boy."

Franny didn't groan, she simply raised her eyes to heaven requisitioning a witness.

"Your father won't hear of it," Madeleine said feebly but fast.

"He's never here to hear of it."

"He's here tonight."

"But you're not."

"Why do you have to have an answer for everything?" asked Madeleine, who'd plumb run out herself.

"You promised."

"I was asleep."

"A promise is a promise."

"A regular Gertrude Stein," her mother mumbled. "Okay," she said, "I accept that. But is a promise a promise when I didn't even hear what I was promising when I promised it?"

"Yes."

"That boy—"

"You said he was nice. You didn't even have to *ask* him to carry your junk."

"It's not junk!"

"He shook hands!"

Beaten, Madeleine unlocked the door. "What's his last name?" she asked.

"Jamie Harris."

Madeleine kissed Franny's peach-soft forehead and stroked back a wisp of hair that had fallen across it. "Finish walking the dog, honey."

"He peed already," Franny said, feeling shaky, as though she wanted to cry—or to bury her face in Madeleine's neck to sniff, as she used to, the special sweet musk that lived in that warm place.

"He needs a run. It's your dog, Franny."

She tore herself away from her mother. "Okay. Come on, Shag. We're going to run—*away from home!*"

"Don't cross the street without looking both ways," Madeleine called automatically, then scolded herself silently. What a ridiculous caution. There was really no way to avoid reality anymore. Franny was —growing up. She sighed and dragged herself and her shopping bags and her attaché case into the house, kicking the door shut behind her.

Corine was at the kitchen sink, snapping string beans and watching the afternoon rerun of "Marcus Welby, M.D."

"We're out of silver polish and Clorox," she said, acknowledging Madeleine's presence.

"Write it down." Madeleine tossed the Bloomingdale's bags into the corner and put her case and purse on the table. "Did you see that boy?" she asked on her way to the kitchen desk.

"He's new."

Madeleine nodded. "Franny's supposed to have a sleep-over with him tomorrow night—" She opened her address book, found the mimeographed school list, and smoothed it out on the desk top, running her finger down the alphabetical listing.

"Well," Corine ventured when the commercial break began, "they're too old to play doctor and too young to do anything else."

"Swell," Madeleine grumbled. "You're a real comfort, Corine." She found the name. "His name is Harris. But his mother's name is Peterfreund—"

Chapter Eleven

The door to Simon's waiting room was open. He was between patients, talking on the phone. "I understand," he was saying, nodding his head understandingly. "I do understand—"

As he spoke, the private line began to ring. He looked up, into the foyer. Barbara, a vase of wilted flowers in her hand, hurried out of the living room to answer it.

"Hello," she said, smiling in at Simon.

"Mrs. Peterfreund?" The voice was unfamiliar, husky but feminine.

"Yes?"

"Hello. I'm Madeleine Philips, Franny Philips's mother—"

Barbara peered through the open door to Simon's office again. "Yes, I understand," he was saying a little more forcefully. He noticed her watching him and smiled back, winking reassurance.

"I understand your son, Jamie, has invited her for a sleep-over at your house tomorrow night."

Tomorrow night? Barbara's heart fluttered with conditioned rage, her face flushing at the intimation of Jamie's night with Ralph, at the thought of Ralph's name, at—that rat!

"Don't apologize," Simon advised on the office phone.

Barbara loved his voice, the way he managed to be

soft-spoken but firm, reassuring without having to coddle or cajole. Most of all, she liked his self-assured assertiveness: a deep, strong sound that wasn't exactly pushy but left no room in which to be pushed around. Taking her cue from him, and without thinking twice about it, she decided to adopt this unusually assertive, secure tone with the woman on the phone who had called that most degrading of memories—her ex-husband—to mind.

"I wouldn't know anything about that," she told Madeleine Philips, each word icy, chipped from the marble of her newfound dignity.

"Pardon?" said Madeleine.

"We'll talk about it tomorrow." Simon Peterfreund was finishing up his conversation.

"Tomorrow," Barbara told the woman on the phone, "Jamie sees his *father*. The entire weekend belongs to—Jamie's father. If you have any questions, I suggest you call Jamie's father." She realized that every time she used the phrase, *Jamie's father*, her voice hit a shrill, spiteful note. She cleared her throat, hoping to regain the deeper tone of forcefulness and control with which she'd started out.

"Good-bye, Mr. Hirschfield," Simon said resonantly. No shilly-shallying about him.

"But—" Madeleine Philips protested.

Well, no shilly-shallying for Mrs. Simon Peterfreund either. "There are no *buts*, Mrs. Philips!"

Simon moved to the door of his office. He listened to her, nodded his head, and winked—as if to say, that's my girl. And his dark mature moustache spread ever so slightly as he smiled approval. Barbara's eyes moistened with pride and love, but she didn't return his smile. No. Resolute, her face as intractable as her voice this time, she continued, "Jamie has two weekends a month with his father, spelled out by the state of New York and my divorce agreement. I have nothing to say about it. That's the way it is."

"Uh—do you happen to have Jamie's father's number?" Madeleine asked cautiously.

"I have his number all right." Barbara permitted herself a little self-congratulatory grin. "His phone number, however, is in the book. Just look up Video-Action and ask for Ralph Harris—the rat. Good-bye, Mrs. Philips." She hung up. Her face burned, but whether it was from embarrassment at her extraordinary outburst, or from pride, she wasn't sure—until Simon put his arm around her.

"Excellent, Barbara," he said proudly. "If you feel it, let it out."

Chapter Twelve

The run from Seventy-fourth to Sixty-ninth Street left both Franny and Shag panting. But for different reasons: Shag was savoring the joy of an exhilarating and unexpected afternoon outing; and, whatever an anxiety attack was, Franny decided she was probably having one. She tried to slow her breathing. The great gulps of city air she'd swallowed trotting through the streets had obviously coursed through her bloodstream and gone to her head and heart, making one light and the other heavy. She held her aching sides and stared at the number 200 etched in stone above the door to a not very impressive old apartment house.

It wasn't exactly a run-down place, but it wasn't anything like what she'd expected—whatever that was. She supposed she thought 200 West Sixty-ninth Street would be a terrific renovated brownstone, that her father would be commuting between two identical homes: his and his. Or maybe she thought it would be a huge old sandblasted building with polished brass poles holding up an elegant awning, a taxi light out front, and hot and cold running doormen. But this place was old and plain and had one of those security system intercoms in a vestibule almost too small to hold a tenant, a dog, and a doorman at the same time.

She'd almost stopped panting. She'd almost decided that Paul didn't, couldn't really live—or even just sleep—in such a place. She decided to take Shag around the block one more time and then go home, to their real and only home. And that was what she did—almost.

She did drag Shag away from the tire he was sniffing and start to run past the building. She did get as far as the corner, in fact. Then she stopped and walked back slowly, back to the building with the stone facade that said 200 and into the ugly little vestibule between the street door and the entrance to the hallway. She ran one finger over the enamel painted wall to the panel of buzzers on which each tenant's name was listed, and then down the list, checking the names until she arrived—with an involuntary intake of breath, a gasp half of surprise, half sorrow—at apartment 8C, where a fresh card had been inserted and on it the name: *P. Philips.*

"This time I got you!" a voice boomed behind her.

Terrified, Franny jumped.

"Out!" the voice commanded. "Out!"

Shag began to bark, and Franny turned to confront an elderly superintendent brandishing a mop. "I've had enough of you rotten kids running in here and pressing all my buttons and getting all my people crazy, so MOVE, you hear?"

Shag's barking became more frenzied, more menacing. He was tugging so hard at the lead that he almost dragged Franny into the super's range. The old man was shouting and using his mop to hold off the dog, and Franny pulled the street door open and bolted. Shag followed her, and so did the voice of the super.

"And I better not see you around here again, or

I'm calling the cops, you hear me? And that goes for the mutt, too!"

When Franny got home, Madeleine's second attempt at establishing communications between the Philips family and the Harris-Peterfreund gang had just terminated. She had spoken to a woman with a melting voice, a regular Nestle's Crunch bar named Fiona, who was Ralph (the rat) Harris's secretary and who had run interference this time.

Madeleine had gotten the Video-Action number from the Manhattan phone book, dialed it, and asked for Harris, minus his ex-wife's honorific, of course. Just plain, "Mr. Ralph Harris, please."

The sweet voice—with a seductive touch of uptown Southern—said that she was sorry, Mr. Harris was on location today—could she take a message.

"When do you expect him back?" Madeleine had asked, and yes, she probably had sounded a bit short. That was when the crispy-crunchys entered Fiona's voice.

"Who is this calling?"

"This is Madeleine Philips, and it's personal, not business. I'm calling about my daughter."

"Oh—"

"And *his* son," she snapped.

Unexpectedly, Fiona's sweetness returned, with a silky ripple of relief running through it. "Oh, Jamie," she said with an affectionate chuckle. "Well, Ralph's out shooting Niagara Falls, but he'll be back by tomorrow night. It's his weekend with Jamie. He picks him up at six."

"He's supposed to pick up my daughter at six-thirty—"

"Not to worry, Mrs. Philips," the secretary cut her

off cheerily. "If he doesn't fall out of the helicopter, he'll be there on the dot. *Ciao!*"

Madeleine blustered a final, "But—" But Fiona had already rung off. And the doorbell was chiming, ding-donging as if it were being rung by an Avon lady in distress. "Nuts," Madeleine muttered, hanging up. Then she started for the hallway, shouting, "All right! I'm coming—"

That was when she heard Franny's voice through the door, plaintive, hysterical, begging, all in one word: *"Ma!"*

She dashed through the foyer and flung open the front door, and Franny, tears streaming down her face, crushed her, held her, and sobbed and shook while every fear known to a New York mother whirled like a Rolodex of *Daily News* headlines through Madeleine's mind.

"My God, Franny—Franny, are you all right? What happened?"

"This man—!" she wailed, remembering the furious superintendent.

"Oh, no!" Madeleine squeezed her and keened, "Oh, my God, no—" She stroked her daughter's unruly hair back from her warm forehead down to the tangled braid behind. "No, no." She stroked the brown suede fringe along the back of Franny's jacket. "Honey—Ssssh—It'll be all right, I promise." She led her sobbing child into the house.

Shag followed them, wagging his tail in gratitude for a good run, capering happily, licking both of them.

"Sssh, honey—I'm your mother, Franny. I love you. You can tell me. Franny, honey, baby, this—man —what—"

"He— He—" Franny hiccuped to a halt. The "man" her mother was asking about was that man—

the superintendent at her father's secret hideaway! Her blue eyes, washed clean with tears, stared up at Madeleine's frightened face. Behind those wide, clear eyes, her brain kicked into high gear, roaring backward through the day's debris for an acceptable substitute, a story that would justify her crying but keep Madeleine's hysteria and the consequences to herself at a minimum.

"He—," she began to improvise, "was in the park."

Her mother's face drained of color. "The park? I told you—How many times have I told you? You don't walk *in* the park. You walk *outside* the park. What happened in the park?"

"At softball—"

Madeleine blinked. "Softball—?"

"This morning—at phys. ed., you know—there was this man in the bushes—with his—" Now what? Was she supposed to be grown up about it or scared into childishness? Should she say "wee-wee" or—

"Penis?" Madeleine offered. Franny nodded. "Oh my God," her mother said, shutting her eyes and holding Franny close again.

"And he was there. He was there—again," Franny concluded. Not bad, really. Only one lie—the "again" part—and she'd crossed her fingers behind her back for that one.

Madeleine took her gently but firmly by the shoulders and held her at arm's length. "Franny," she said with a seriousness that seemed almost ceremonial, "did he touch you?"

"No."

"Thank God," her mother breathed barely audibly. Then she managed a smile. It was a tight, sort of phony little smile, but Franny was grateful for it. "Fran, Franny, darling—That's a sad, sick, unhappy

man, and he needs help. I want you to put it out of
your mind. I want you to think of something beautiful and wonderful and fun that will make you happy—"

"Like the sleep-over?"

Madeleine sighed but acquiesced. "Yes. Like the
sleep-over," she said. "Tomorrow. With Jamie."

Book Two
Grown-ups

Chapter Thirteen

Madeleine phoned Steven Sloan at his law firm. She was in the lobby of the Isaac and Yetta Moscowitz Memorial Hall for Senior Citizens. It was well past six when she decided to call, so she used his night-line number and, happily, he was still there. He picked up after seven rings, and he sounded a little foggy.

"Steve?"

"Mmmmm."

"Were you napping?"

"Uh-uh—Madeleine?" His voice cleared. "Hi. What's up?" he asked cheerfully.

"Dinner tomorrow evening, if you'd like."

"Tomorrow? Friday. Great. The usual place okay,

or are you feeling particularly adventurous?"

"*Chez moi*," she said.

"Your house? Oh, you mean you *and* Paul—"

"No. Just us."

"At your place? You're kidding," he said with a touch of uneasiness utterly alien to his exquisitely cool facade.

There was rarely anything that shocked or even surprised Steven Sloan. He was bright, successful, easygoing, and attractive. More attractive, Madeleine (who was no slouch herself) had always felt, than a bright, successful, easygoing married man had any right to be. He had a quirky, boyish grin that made you feel anger was silly and sadness utterly unnecessary. He had a way of fixing his lazy-lidded blue eyes on you that made you want to settle out of court.

"You're not kidding." He'd laughed the trace of uneasiness off quickly. "What about Franny?"

"She's got a sleep-over date—er—appointment."

"Hold on a sec," Steve said, and she'd heard him talking to someone who'd obviously come into his office. He'd either put his hand over the mouthpiece of the phone or had it pressed against his chest. "Mad," he'd said after a moment. "Things are wild here. I've got to get back. What time tomorrow?"

"Eight, eight-thirty."

"We're on."

Paul was not so delighted about the sleep-over.

They sat, at 6:25 on Friday—Paul, Franny, Madeleine—stiffly, as if American Gothic had exchanged a pitchfork for an angelic-looking twelve-year-old girl, watching the clock and waiting.

Occasionally Paul broke rank to pace to the window and back. Each time he did, he glanced with contempt at the little overnight bag perched on the

oak cabinet in the hallway and then glanced back,
condemnatory and stiffer than ever, at Madeleine.

"Do you have an umbrella? Does she have an umbrella?" he demanded.

Franny shook her head, no. Madeleine smiled com-
fortingly at her. "You look very beautiful, Bubbs,"
she said. "Haven't seen you out of jeans since nursery
school, I think."

"You look very pretty," Paul snapped, as if Madeleine's compliment had been meant to show him up,
show him lacking in parental sensitivity. "What's his
name again?"

"Jamie Harris."

"The kid whose parents are 'split,' right?" Paul put
on the glasses he sometimes wore and started pacing
again. He glared at Madeleine. "The kid whose parents are so self-involved that they send him to school
dressed like an oddball, right?"

"Oh, daddy!" Franny cried. She ran past him down
the hall to the bathroom.

"For goodness sake, Paul," Madeleine said. "They're
only twelve years old, and they're going to be with
his father!"

"And what do you know about his father?"

That he'll show up if his helicopter doesn't crash,
and that his ex-wife can't mention his name without
calling him a rat, Madeleine thought morosely.

Paul stalked back to the window. Yellow leaves
lay scattered on the slick dark street, floating in pud-
dles lighted by the new mugger-deterrent lamps for
which the neighborhood association had fought City
Hall. The block was wet and lovely, shimmering in
the vaguely greenish glow of the lights. Quiet and
peaceful, Paul thought. He loved this street, this
place—his home. Of course, there was always someone flashy who had to gun his motor to get a little

attention, he thought, annoyed at the sound and sight of a bright yellow Maserati cruising the street. It seemed to be searching for a parking place and, finally—bearing out the premonition that had set his teeth on edge only a second before—the sleek low-slung little Italian car double-parked in front of his house.

Like an obscene invitation, the headlights, as provocative and obtrusive as Giancarlo Giannini's eyes, lowered seductively and disappeared into the sloping front end.

A man got out of the car, a young-looking man wearing jeans, a tie-less shirt, and a soft brown leather jacket. The wind tossed his hair, which was long enough to curl over the back of his jacket collar, Paul noted. Then he realized, with a sense of reprieve, that the Maserati was a two-seater and that the second seat was filled with legs—two long feminine legs covered at the upper thighs by a slinky pale purple thing. The couple had obviously made a mistake and parked, or double-parked, at the wrong house, on the wrong block. The man in the leather jacket pushed his seat forward, and Jamie Harris, the kid who'd mumbled hello to Franny in front of the school yesterday, crawled out.

"Okay. That's it. They're here," Paul muttered. "He's driving a Maserati." It was an accusation.

Madeleine stood and smoothed the waistline of her tailored tweed jacket. She glanced down the hall. "I'm tired, Paul," she said softly. "I am tired of playing 'Let's Pretend.'"

"A Maserati—in a city where you can't drive over fifteen miles an hour."

"I am tired of this insane overprotective structure that you are imposing on our lives."

"And he won't even buy the kid a pair of blue jeans." Paul shook his head sadly.

Outside, Ralph Harris was brushing the shoulders of his son's blue blazer and pretending to straighten the tie Jamie wore tucked inside his crew neck sweater. "Hey, it's our first double date," he called as his son started for the Philips's front door. He looked the house over approvingly. "Not bad, huh?" he asked Donna, the leggy blonde stewardess in the front seat.

"Cute," she said.

"Cute?"

"Jamie."

"Oh." Ralph smiled. "I meant the house."

Donna's eyes widened with disbelief. "You wouldn't catch me living in it. I mean, no doorman. You could get killed—"

Jamie rang the bell.

"How could you let her go?" Paul hissed at Madeleine.

"I promised."

"Promised!" He stalked to the entryway to answer the door.

"If you don't want her to go, *you* do something about it," Madeleine called after him.

"Hi, Mr. Philips," Jamie said amiably.

"Hello, Jamie."

"Is Franny ready?"

Franny came swiftly down the hall and picked up her overnight bag from the cabinet. She was reaching to lift her jacket from the bentwood coat stand when Paul said, "I'd like to meet your father, Jamie," and closed the door.

"Daa-ddy!" she groaned. And she set her bag down again.

"Paul—," Madeleine said in a similar tone.

"Oh, ma! They've got to think I am some kind of *infant*—"

"They will know that your father has some concern about you." Paul smiled lovingly at her.

"Whereas your mother, of course—," said Madeleine, rising to the bait.

"I wouldn't blame them if they just took off," Franny said miserably.

The doorbell rang again. Paul winked at Franny as he went to answer it. "Faint heart never won fair lady."

She looked to Madeleine who tried to smile reassuringly but couldn't quite. Franny's look said, what are we going to do about him? Madeleine's fading smile answered, I don't know. They sat down on the sofa together and stared gloomily at the wall.

Paul opened the door. "Ralph Harris," said Ralph Harris, extending his hand.

"Paul Philips."

"Good to meet you—"

"I thought we should meet," Paul said, breaking in awkwardly, "before you kidnap my daughter."

"Kidnap—?" Ralph chuckled weakly and glanced at Jamie who found something to stare at on the ceiling. "I should have thought of it myself."

Paul led Ralph Harris to the living room, sizing up every detail of his clothing and carriage. He knew the type—from the scuffed Gucci loafers (from which Harris had coyly removed the telltale buckles) to the wide-strapped wristwatch that did everything but make toast. He probably hadn't worn a tie in ten years and considered it an accomplishment, too.

"Video-Action. TV commercials, right?"

"Yeah. Not for much longer, though. I'm planning to do a feature soon—"

Right, Paul thought. The guy's never directed anything that runs longer than sixty seconds, but he considers himself an *auteur*.

"That's quite a car."

"It's transportation."

"Subways are transportation."

They entered the living room, Jamie trailing by a foot or so. "This is quite a house."

"Thanks. My wife—," Paul began as Madeleine uncrossed her legs and started to rise. Ralph spotted her ankles first, appreciated the legs, and then, a connoisseur, the whole package. "—put a lot of herself into it," Paul concluded crisply. He'd noticed Ralph's appraisal of Madeleine, and he didn't appreciate it. He also noticed that she'd noticed—and did appreciate it. "This is Jamie's father," he said to Madeleine.

"Ralph Harris," said Ralph, cutting Paul short.

"Madeleine," she said, taking his hand.

"I'm Franny."

"Hi, Franny."

"Can I get you a drink?" Madeleine asked.

"Have you got everything?" Jamie asked Fran.

"Thanks, but I'm double-parked."

"I'm all ready," Franny said. "Let's go."

Jamie touched his father's sleeve. "She's ready."

Ralph looked from Madeleine to Paul and back again. "Okay?"

The children moved toward the hall. There was an uneasy silence while Madeleine waited for Paul to say something. When Paul didn't, and a truck horn began to honk urgently outside, she said, "Fine."

A second horn, a bit shriller, joined the truck. Ralph recognized it. Donna was blowing the Maserati's horn back at the truck driver. "Oh, no—" he said, visions of scraped fenders and bloodied blondes obliterating the strained smile on his face.

"So long, everybody," Franny called.

Madeleine followed her to the hall. "Kiss?"

Franny kissed her. Jamie opened the front door. "It's a truck," he told Ralph.

"I forgot my bag," Franny said over the cacophony of horns.

"And your father." Paul handed her the little overnight case. He looked misty-eyed, sad and serious. It seemed a long time since she'd seen him truly laugh or smile. Even their morning tickles were no longer honest. She put her arms around him, feeling almost as lonely as he looked, and kissed him good-bye.

"Hang on. Keep your shirt on!" Ralph shouted to the truck driver as Franny and Jamie rushed toward the car. "We'll take good care of her," he promised Madeleine as he raced down the steps. "Don't worry."

"I'm not worried," Paul said, watching the kids scramble into the tiny back seat.

"If you're worried," Madeleine said, "why didn't you *say* something?"

"You say things. You're the one who says things in the morning that you can't even remember in the afternoon."

"How can I remember when I can't get a night's sleep because my bed is invaded at dawn?" Then they both waved, Madeleine and Paul, standing side by side in the doorway, hollow smiles set on their faces.

"Martians could invade that bed and all you'd do is roll over and snore."

"I don't snore," she said firmly, smiling.

"See that?" Paul pointed to the car and the children. "Take a good look. That, in a nutshell, is divorce." He smiled and waved.

"What in a nutshell?"

"That pathetic, inhibited kid."

"He shook hands. He says, How do you do."

"He can't even look me in the eye," Paul insisted.

"You're six feet tall!"

They waved until the Maserati opened its jaundiced eyes again and roared off into the night. Paul's smile-locked face unlocked at last. "How could you let her go?"

Madeleine stared at the new face that was becoming provocatively familiar—the bittersweet, sad, spanked puppy-dog face of Paul Philips. Slowly, deliberately, she answered his question: "I want the night off. And the morning!" Then she turned on her heels and went inside.

He followed immediately. "Ah, ha!"

She started up the stairs to the second floor.

"That's it. At last," he shouted, two steps behind her. "You, you, you, you—"

"You agreed to a separation." She cut him off at the second *you*, but he sputtered on until what she'd said sunk in.

"I did it," he said then. "I sublet the apartment—"

"You're never in it! You're here every morning, you eat dinner here, you spend the whole weekend here—I see more of you than I did when we were married!"

"We are married!" he reminded her, backing into the wall as she whirled on him.

"I want a divorce. I want a nice, intelligent, *angry* divorce like everybody else I know."

"You've got it!"

"*And Franny!*" they both shouted at once.

Then Madeleine, tears of rage nearly blinding her, ran up the stairs to change and prepare for her evening with Steven Sloan. Paul, patting his vest pocket to be sure he had the opera tickets with him, ran down the stairs, grabbed his raincoat, and slammed out of the house, determined not to subject sweet young Carolyn Reid to another morose lecture on failed marriage.

He'd only known Carolyn for a couple of weeks, but she was the kind of girl you could really talk to. She was new to the city, just arrived from Wisconsin, and nothing bored her. She was eager to listen and learn and see everything. She was also blonde, blue-eyed, soft-spoken, and innocent—a condition he assumed was indigenous, epidemic for all he knew, among Wisconsin youth. And, as the almost ex-husband of the native New York harridan upstairs, he, for one, was grateful. As he sloshed toward Lincoln Center to meet Carolyn Reid, he vowed he'd never eat another piece of domestic cheese again without paying homage to the great Dairy State that produced her.

He arrived early and circled the fountain at the center of the plaza. The wind swept a spray of water on him, and he patted his face with one of the freshly ironed handkerchiefs Corine had left in his dresser drawer. To Paul, that handkerchief symbolized everything that was right about marriage. The sweet, clean smell of it; the fact that it had been laid neatly in its proper place in his dresser drawer, so that it was there when he needed it. That was what a good marriage should be like.

Paul tucked the damp handkerchief into his pocket, and when he looked up again he noticed a couple crossing the plaza, heading toward the opera house. The moustached man had his arm around the petite woman with short windblown reddish hair. They were talking softly, passionately; not arguing, but talking. They were very definitely married. You could tell just by looking at them. They probably had been for years, but they still knew how to communicate lovingly, he thought with a pang of envy.

The woman was Barbara Peterfreund. "I try, Simon," she was saying. "You heard me say, Good night, Melody."

"I know."

"She won't say a word."

"Come January she's off to college."

"Maybe she'll say good-bye," Barbara ventured. He squeezed her reassuringly, and she continued. "And Jamie can't wait to tear off with his father every other Friday night."

"It's perfectly normal for a boy to want to see his father—"

"He makes comparisons between Ralph and me," she said quickly. She didn't want to hear about normalcy now. "And you want to know the truth? The truth is, he likes Ralph better."

"It's not true," Simon said.

"How do you know?"

"Every other *Sunday* night, he comes back to you."

"To us, Simon." She stared up at him adoringly.

Lovers, Paul thought; married, adult, but filled with obvious passion and respect for one another. Lovers.

"Right," Simon said. "Come on, darling, the Katzes are waiting."

Chapter Fourteen

Franny and Jamie sat across from Ralph and Donna. The table was in the rear of an Eastside restaurant where the bartender and at least one waiter (not the one serving their table) knew Ralph.

The table in the back room was covered with a red and white checkered tablecloth. A lighted candle was stuck in the straw-covered Chianti bottle, and their waiter had brought a basket of breadsticks and their drinks—scotch for Ralph, white wine for Donna, Cokes for Jamie and Fran. On one side of the table was a narrow service aisle; on the other side was a chicken-wire fence that separated the dining area from a bocce court. The restaurant was Il Vagabondo, though Ralph dropped the formal *Il* whenever he mentioned the name.

"What do you think of Vagabondo?" he'd asked Franny who was genuinely captivated by the strange little dirt-floored bowling court that occupied most of the back room.

"Neat."

Ralph beamed. "*Salud!*" he said, clinking his scotch against their Cokes.

In the candle glow, which was supplemented by fairly bright overhead lighting, he looked older than he had in her living room, Franny thought. He had panda eyes, deep brown, maybe even black, surrounded by circles darker than the rest of his face,

which was either suntanned or colored by one of
those men's bronzing lotions. The discolored skin
around his eyes was lined with tired-looking pouches.
But his smile was young.

And he smiled, really truly deep-down smiled,
whenever he looked over at Jamie. Franny noticed
that. Someday Paul would smile like that again at
her. Someday, she and Paul and some girl—but
please, not a life-sized Barbie Doll like the purple
and blonde stewardess blinking up at Ralph—would
be out to dinner together and he'd smile at her with
the pride and love so evident in Jamie's father's
smile. But she doubted that she'd ever call her father
Paul the way Jamie called his *Ralph*.

"That's just the cutest thing," Donna said, pointing
a fingernail, painted the same color as her dress, at
Franny's little pink ceramic pin shaped like a man's
tie.

"Thanks—uh, your nails are neat, too."

Donna blinked and smiled. "They match," she said.
She had beautiful white teeth, flawed only by a smear
of purple lip gloss that Franny wanted to tell her
about but decided it might be impolite. Definitely
put-your-money-where-your-mouth-is teeth: the kind
that made you come swooning home from a date to
tell your roommate she'd had the right idea about
toothpaste all along.

Donna's eyes were wide, blue, and expressive of a
limited variety of feelings: appreciation, gratitude, and
lack of understanding—the last was usually preceded
by two blinks of her black beaded All-Night lashes,
followed by an utterly blank wide-eyed stare.

"Have you ever been in a crash?" Jamie asked her.

A fourth feeling was added to the blue-eyed reper-
toire: terror.

"No, thank goodness." Donna crossed herself and

giggled nervously. "We did hit one terrible air pocket a few weeks ago though. That's how I met your father." Donna smiled from Jamie to Ralph.

"With a full tray," Ralph added.

"I didn't spill a thing."

"Puerto Rico," he reminded Jamie. "The rain forest shoot."

Donna's smooth brow creased with seriousness. She pointed a breadstick at the children. "That's why, even if the seat belt sign isn't on, you really have to stay fastened in. Have you ever been on an airplane?" she asked.

Franny felt Jamie's knee jamming hers under the table. They stared at her as if she were crazy but politely nodded their assent to her strange question. Then, hidden behind their menus, they exchanged groaning glances.

The waiter came by for their order. Franny and Jamie decided to stick with spaghetti and meatballs, but Ralph talked Donna into trying the manicotti and, for himself, he ordered ossobuco. Donna said it sounded like the latest Latin disco sound. She flew in and out of Miami a lot.

The spaghetti was fun. Franny and Jamie were zupping it up, laughing when the sauce gathered at the corners of their mouths or when a lank strand whiplashed a lip, leaving a bloody streak of marinara in its wake.

Donna picked at her manicotti, her face trying to keep its cheery aspect while her eyes blinked their distress code. "It's all cheesy," she confided to Ralph, and after a couple of weak attempts to swallow the stuff, she set her fork down daintily and turned back to Franny and Jamie, wincing at the sound and sight of their splashing spaghetti sauce.

"Now tell me," she said with exquisite condescension, "where all you've been to—"

"London," Jamie said, whirling a fresh sheaf of spaghetti onto his fork.

"Paris," said Franny.

"Paris—S—San Francisco," Jamie said, deciding to switch, without warning, to the game of Geography.

San Francisco. *O*, thought Franny. The object was for each new place to begin with the last letter of the place before. "Ohio," she said.

"Ochos Rios."

"Och*o* Ri*o*." Ralph caught on and corrected Jamie's pronunciation.

"San Francisco," Franny said.

"I said that before."

"Oh—Stamford."

"Denmark."

"*K*—*K* for Kansas. You were right. It's Topeka." They cracked up, giggling and trying to contain the spaghetti sauce spray at the same time.

"Alaska," Jamie sputtered. He covered his mouth with his hand, a habit he'd adopted since he'd gotten the braces but which he'd just about broken. However, the sauce and meatball bits necessitated it now.

"Gross." Franny laughed. "Arabia."

"Alabama."

Donna turned to Ralph. "I guess it's silly to ask these days," she said weakly.

"They're just playing a game," he assured her.

Her lips formed a perfect, purple *O*. "What time do they go to bed?" she asked.

After the meal, Ralph attempted to teach the children to play bocce. Donna, who'd declined the invitation to join them, sat, alternately sipping the American coffee she'd ordered and the licorice-tasting

Sambuca—a colorless liqueur served with three coffee
beans floating in it like dead cockroaches—he'd ordered for her. She watched glumly through the chick-
en wire.

The first thing they had to learn was that the game,
which was pronounced "bah-chee," was spelled
b-o-c-c-e. Then Ralph gave Franny and Jamie each a
bocce ball—a wooden ball similar in intent to an
American bowling ball but smaller, made of hard-
wood, and without finger holes.

"Like in *boule*," Franny said.

"*Boule?*"

"Sure. When we were in southern France we
watched a bunch of old men playing a game just like
this. Only they called it *boule*."

"Right," Ralph said. Then he sent them to the far
end of the court while he threw out an even smaller
wooden ball—a red one—which was the marker they
were to aim for. He walked to the side of the court
and smiled at Donna, who curled a finger through the
chicken wire to touch his hand. "A looker," he said,
pointing with his chin to the kids at the other end. "A
couple of years, she'll be a knockout. Like her old lady."

"Mmmm," Donna mused, running her hand through
the side of her hair that bore the diamond imprints of
the wire fence.

Franny looked over at them. "Are they always like
that?" she asked Jamie.

"Like what?"

"The women."

"You never know."

"How do you stand it?"

"You get used to it," he explained. "I grade them.
She's a *C* minus."

Ralph was coming toward them. "What are we supposed to do now?" Franny asked him pleasantly.

"Just watch me. It's a cinch." He took one of the balls. "Now watch, Franny. The whole thing is in the wrist—" He tossed the ball down the court toward the red marker. His form was great. He looked graceful. He ended his pitch a bit like an Ice Capades skater dipping cross-legged to the crowd. The ball missed the marker by about two feet.

"The object is to get as close to the marker as possible," Jamie said. "Or just blow it away, so it's as far from your opponent's ball as possible."

Franny threw. Her pitch landed between Ralph's ball and the marker; closer to the marker than to Ralph's ball.

"How about bowling?" Ralph asked.

Jamie threw. His ball practically blew the marker out of the park.

"Do you like to bowl?" Ralph was asking Franny. "American style?"

"It's okay."

"Well, okay then! Let's go. This is just kid stuff anyway, right?"

"Bowling?" Donna blinked twice. "I mean on a Friday night in New York City?—I mean, like—uh—how? Where?"

Ralph knew just the place. And after bowling (boys against girls, Ralph insisted, until Donna twisted her ankle and had to hobble from the game) they all went to Baskin-Robbins for ice cream, and Ralph insisted that Donna try the bubble gum flavor. It took two licks and a "Yuch!" before the entire scoop tumbled off the cone and careened down her body, landing in a blob on the tip of one of her sandals—the sandal whose strap was opened to accommodate her slightly swollen ankle.

For Donna, the evening went downhill from there. It started to rain when they were halfway between

Baskin-Robbins and the Maserati, and her hair drooped—defeated, drowned. Only her All-Night mascara stood the test. Everything else, including her sunny disposition, seemed to be getting rained out. Her smile had become a forlorn grimace, white-toothed and turned up at the edges, but the dazzle was definitely gone. That she could try to smile at all was a wonder. It warmed Franny's heart and piqued her guilt to see such a plucky loser.

The pretty young stewardess's teeth were chattering by the time Ralph manipulated the Maserati into a tiny parking space opposite the small building on East Sixty-second Street in which he lived. He parked between a limo with diplomatic plates and a Mercedes sedan with a discreet MD license. Franny and Jamie, released from the confines of the back seat, were bursting with energy. They waited impatiently on the curb for the traffic to clear.

"I feel like a pretzel," Franny said.

"Come on. Race you to the door."

"My foot's asleep."

Jamie laughed. "Okay. Hop you to the door."

Donna, damp, chilled, and trembling in the drizzly wake of the downpour, stared at them as if they were Martians. Ralph was locking the car.

"Hey," he called when he noticed them hopping in the gutter, "watch yourselves!" They ran the rest of the way. He put the car keys in his pocket and took Donna's arm.

"Uh—I think I'll go home and get into some hot rollers," she said softly.

"You look great," he said.

She smiled. Her eyes were wide; grateful but unconvinced. "I have this little teeny headache," she said. "And this hair."

Ralph started to steer her across the street. "We'll go upstairs. The kids'll go to sleep. We'll have a nice quiet drink."

She cringed. "We just had ice cream. It—uh—dripped on me, and I know it's going to leave a stain. So far tonight we had this food I don't eat, and bocce I don't play, and real bowling where I twisted my foot, and Baskin-Robbins that dripped all over me—"

"How's your foot?" Ralph asked sympathetically. But Donna was rolling along on her own steam now.

"And my hair—" she continued, "just forget it. So the way things are going, I don't want a drink because I'll probably choke on it. I think I'll just go home and see if I can get this stain out and soak my foot and put my hair up—"

"Donna, I'm really sorry."

"It's not your fault."

He looked across the street at the children waiting in the vestibule of his building. "I told her father I'd watch out for her," he said sadly.

She kissed him lightly. "I'll call you," she said.

Ralph held her frail arm. He looked back at Jamie and Franny standing in the well-lighted, warm and dry little hallway. "Well—they're here. I mean, what's going to happen to them alone in an apartment for five minutes—or ten? Now don't move," he cautioned Donna. "I'll be right back."

He hurried across to the building and trotted up the steps. "Jamie—," he began, entering the vestibule.

"It's okay," Jamie said. "I've got the key."

"I'll take her home, and then I'll put the car in the garage. I won't be late," his father said. "But you don't have to wait up."

Jamie nodded.

"Thank you for the dinner and the bowling, Mr. Harris."

Ralph's eyes softened. "You're welcome, honey," he told Franny. "Sleep tight."

They waited until he'd helped Donna back into the car and started up the motor. Jamie shook his head. "She gets a *D*," he said. "Definitely a *D*." He unlocked the door and led Franny into the little elevator at the rear of the building and pressed 4, which was the top floor.

"We have to take our shoes off," he told her as the elevator doors opened onto a mirrored hall decorated in a vaguely oriental motif.

"Why?"

"You'll see." His face was secretive, which was not odd, but there was a glimmer of excitement and satisfaction in it, of fun, which was rare, and special. Franny almost giggled with the curiosity his disguised matter-of-factness stirred in her. She took off her damp suede sandals and put them beside his shoes under the lacquered Japanese table in the hall.

"You do this every time?"

Jamie nodded.

"And nobody steals them?"

"Nope," he said. He waited until she'd straightened up, and he put his key in the door. She could almost hear him counting to himself: one, two, three, go; then he turned the key and pushed the door open. She gasped.

Directly before them was a lush garden, a magical jungle. Fountains, and birds—some in ornate cages, others perched live and free on the branches of dwarfed tropical trees and hanging plants—all under a greenhouse roof. It wasn't a simple city skylight, but an elaborate glass ceiling—on the fourth floor of a

very ordinary apartment building—shimmering with
the pink glow, yellow-white lights, and wondrous silhouette of the New York skyline surrounding it. Rain
tapped delicately on the roof glass. Clouds, reflecting the glow below, changed shape in spectral shift-
ing layers and drifted lazily overhead like phantom
balloons from some long-ago Macy's Thanksgiving
Day parade.

The entrance to this extraordinary garden was a
rainbow: a brightly painted wooden arch from which
there dangled, like harem beads, strips of film—
black celluloid strips with perforated edges—that rattled as Jamie put his hand through the odd divider
to press the light switch. And then, absurdly, marvel-
ously, an ornate Venetian chandelier that had nothing to do with the garden, the film strips, or the delicately woven Japanese mats that covered the floor,
glittered to life, sparkling and dancing against the
breathtaking reflected light of New York at night.

Jamie watched Franny as she moved through the
celluloid strips. He listened to the sharp intake of her
breath as the wonders surrounding her were multiplied by the new sights and textures and colors within. The chandelier lights glinted on the metal of
Jamie's braces as a wide smile split his secretive self
and opened his whole face with pride and delight in
her pleasure.

"You like it?"

"It's—"

"Neat?" he finished for her.

She turned to face him; her eyes were bright, alive
with near-feverish excitement. "It's—Shaggylon," she
whispered.

They explored the rest of the apartment together.
Shoji screens separated the living room–garden from
the rest of the place, so each room could be discov-

ered individually, at leisure, or in little uncontrollable bursts of enthusiasm that Franny could not contain. Jamie, familiar with the wonders of Ralph's domain, regained his cool facade, but there was no doubt that Franny's growing amazement pleased him immensely and that he wanted to introduce her to more unexpected treasures.

"This is Saki." A beautiful white bird, large and majestic, jumped from a perch onto Jamie's hand. Franny held out her hand, and the creature hopped onto it.

"Nice Saki," she crooned as the bird flew off, back into the jungle.

"You ever seen piranhas?" Jamie asked. They were examining one of several brightly lighted fish tanks that glowed out of the strategically designed darkness.

"They eat people," Franny said.

"Yeah. You gotta be real careful." Jamie dipped his hand into the tank, yelled "Ouch!" and pulled his hand out again, minus his forefinger.

"Jamie!" she shrieked.

He laughed and opened his hand to reveal the hidden finger.

"Oooo, you!" Laughing, they continued to circle the room. They passed and touched and stared at a funhouse mirror, a slot machine, and a glittering black snake slithering calmly along a low-hanging tree branch.

"I don't believe it," Franny said at last.

"There's more."

"Wait," she called as he was about to pull back one of the Japanese screens that divided the rooms. She sat down and pulled off her socks. Then she stood and curled her toes on the exquisitely soft tatami mat, reveling in the sensation. Jamie watched for a

while, then slid open the shoji screen to reveal the
dining room: a low lacquered table surrounded by
Japanese backrests; an aquarium wall; and a quiet
niche in which sat a small Buddha filled with incense.

"This is where Ralph meditates," Jamie explained,
kneeling before the shrine and ceremoniously lighting
a joss stick. "He works a lot in Japan—"

Franny knelt beside him and inhaled the incense
romantically. And sneezed.

"Come on," he said, pulling her to her feet. He led
her to a hallway, a mirrored tunnel, in fact, where
myriad Frannys stood gaping, and they were almost
unable to tell which one was real. He led her slowly
through the tunnel allowing her to turn and watch her
image bounce from every wall.

The bedroom made her laugh aloud. "Oh, no. Oh
Jamie!" She ran to the center of the room where a
huge sunken water bed was set serenely amidst the
electronic neon madness all around them. She threw
herself onto the bed and floated crazily on top of it.

The room was surrounded by mirrors that opened
at odd angles to reveal closets and hidden bureaus
and linen cabinets. There was even a mirror above
the bed in which Franny watched herself flying to
and fro, up and down, on the water bed.

Somewhere to the left of the sunken bed was a real
jukebox—all lit up in orange, red, and blue—and a
blue neon skyline, a sculpture, Jamie called it, mount-
ed on the small bit of brick wall left unmirrored.
There was another lighted sculpture that looked just
like a department store dummy—a torso, from neck
to upper thigh, on which a blouse or T-shirt might
be displayed—except that it was made of translucent
white plastic and lit somehow from within. It sat,
glowing, on the platform that surrounded the bed.

Behind the warm rippling bed was an enormous

black bathtub, about six by six feet square, with several ornate waterspouts scattered at intervals inside it. Franny leaped from the bed to the rim of the tub, her bare feet absorbing the coolness of the polished stone.

"Is it marble?"

"Mica, I think. It's a kind of plastic-y mineral stuff —," he mumbled vaguely. "Like Lucite or something."

"It's cool," Franny said. Jamie made a face at the word. "I mean really cool, you know, like in 'cold' cool." She pointed to the several spouts inside the tub. "What's all that for? What's it do besides hot and cold?"

"It's a Jacuzzi," he said. "A Jacuzzi whirlpool. Water comes out of all those fixtures. You can adjust the temperature and the spray. And it kind of massages you all over."

"You've done it?"

"What?"

"Fooled around in here—"

"Sure," Jamie said.

She thought she could see his face flush with the strange shyness that surfaced now and again, but with all the hot colors reflecting from the mirrors, it was hard to tell reality from fantasy. An embarrassed blush might merely be a reflection of the pink glow of the extraordinary neon towel rack beside the tub.

Jamie spun another mirrored panel. "Watch this." He stood with his right side hidden behind the mirror, his left side reflected in it. Then he bent his left leg at the knee and lifted it off the floor. His entire body seemed to be suspended in air, caught jumping, floating miraculously.

"That's terrific! Let me try—"

"Wait," he told her. "This is the special panel—the *sacred* one."

Franny automatically put her hand to her mouth, waiting, holding her breath, almost literally, with tingling fingertips, as Jamie slowly finished rotating the mirrored panel. Then she fell back onto, into, the bed, and she cracked up, laughing.

Behind the mirror was a life-size black-and-white portrait of Ralph, fully dressed in his shirt, jeans, and Gucci loafers. His hands were joined, palm to palm, in sublime meditation. And he was grinning beatifically. His eyes shone with benevolent mischief down into the pit that held the huge water bed.

Franny rolled on the bed, giggling, until she finally collapsed, awestruck and almost speechless. "Where," she gasped, "did it all come from?"

"Commercials," Jamie said. He crossed to an area that looked like the control room aboard the starship *Enterprise*. It was a built-in wall unit, a bookcase filled with video-cassette tapes, flanking the enormous screen of an Advent television. Jamie gestured to the cassette library. "He makes them."

"Those are all commercials?"

"All over the world."

Franny sat up. The bed rocked, and she floated cross-legged on the comfortably quilted tide. "We don't even watch them," she said. "My mom just clicks them off."

"They're better than the programs and they're harder to do," Jamie said decisively.

"They're awful," said Franny.

Jamie's normally neutral face was definitely flushed now. His voice, however, was cool. "You know what you have to do in thirty seconds?" he demanded with icy authority. "You have to tell a story and you have

to sell a product and you have to get *production*
values. Go ahead, count to thirty and try it, if
you're so smart."

"How am I supposed to know?"

"You'd know if you used your brain, stupid."

She clamored out of the bed. "I am not stupid."

"You don't know anything," Jamie said with disgust.

"Oh, yes, I do."

"What?" She was heading for the hall and Jamie
was following her. "What do you know? Go on, tell
me, one thing. What do you know?"

She spun around to face him. "I want to go home!"
Then she turned back and rushed into the living
room. Angry and determined, she found her socks
and started to put them on.

Jamie watched her. He said nothing, but the color
in his cheeks heightened, and his eyes, though he
strained to keep them calm looking, misted. He
clenched his jaw and swallowed back the awful full-
ness in his throat. When he was certain that his voice
could be trusted to remain factual and calm, he said,
"You can't."

"I can to," she said hotly, hopping around on one
foot trying to slip into her second sock.

"Your father isn't sleeping there," Jamie reminded
her dryly. "If you go home, they'll know that you
know he isn't sleeping there, and it'll be a big mess.
And how do you even know your mother's there?"

Her sock half on, Franny stopped. "I don't," she
said softly.

Jamie put his hands over his eyes as if he were
weary. He took a deep breath before he let his hands
fall to his sides again. "You want a Coke?" he asked
gently.

She shook her head, no.

"We can watch the late show."

She didn't respond.

"Franny—"

She couldn't look at him. She was staring down at her feet, the second sock dangling from her hand. "What?" she asked finally.

"I—uh, I don't know what your father does either." It was as close to an apology as he could come.

"He's a consultant," she said flatly.

"To what?"

She pulled off her sock. "To business." She tied the two socks into a loose knot, the way Corine always did after she'd laundered them. "He tells people how to run their business."

"Why?"

"So they make more money. He tells them how to make money. My mom tells them how to save money. And he voted for President Ford and she voted for Carter, and maybe that's why they have problems."

"Ralph hates what he does," Jamie confessed. "He clicks them off, too. He says they're just lousy, crumby TV commercials. He says it's all garbage."

Franny looked over at him. He was staring down at his feet, unable to face her.

"Is that why—" she began. She wanted to say *Is that why you got so angry at me before?* "It must—" she tried again. She'd started to say *It must be lonely,* but what she'd meant was, *It must be lonely and hard to be proud of your father's work when even he puts it down.* She stopped trying to speak and was grateful when Jamie, giving no indication that he'd heard her mumbled starts and stops, continued on his own.

"He's moving to California—" His voice was thick and bitter. "To make a feature." The word *feature* sounded like a direct quote from Ralph. Even the

style and rhythm of Jamie's speech had taken on a
professional-sounding bitterness, a disillusioned
grown-up's voice. But the thickness was young, younger by far than Jamie's everyday voice, and vulnerable.
It was the sort of thickness that preceded tears.

"Feature?"

"Movie. A feature's a movie."

"When?" she asked quietly.

"Soon."

"Will he live there?"

Jamie shrugged. "I guess."

"When will you—?" She became quickly aware of a
note of panic in her voice. It was her own father
she was thinking of, not Jamie's. Would Paul move
away, too—three *thousand miles* away? She cleared
her throat and tried to concentrate on Jamie's problem. "When will you see him?" she asked in a more
measured tone.

"Christmas. The summer. He says he'll be back and
forth a lot." Jamie looked up briefly. "He says he has
to." He looked away again.

Instinctively, Franny's hand reached toward him.
She pulled it back, and it clenched, all on its own,
into an angry little fist. For some reason, the fist wanted to punch that sublimely smiling blowup of Ralph
that was hanging in the bedroom.

"Do you want a Coke?" she asked Jamie. When he
didn't answer, she said, "Let's watch the late show."

Chapter Fifteen

Madeleine leaned across the table and absently picked a piece of blonde hair off the shoulder of Steven Sloan's black crew neck sweater.

"He wants Franny," she told him.

There were low candles on the dining table. A few slices of French bread, no longer warm, were still wrapped in the linen napkin she'd placed inside the straw basket. There was a bit of salad left. And two earthenware bowls—hers half full, his bearing only the dregs of the chili she'd made that he'd always liked. He'd brought the wine, and they were on their second bottle now.

Steve glanced with amusement at the blonde hair she toyed with and then, mindlessly tossed away. He placed his hand over hers when it was empty again.

"And—?" he asked.

"No," Madeleine said. "He can't have her. No." She pulled a cigarette from the pack beside her salad plate. He lit it.

"There's joint custody. There are a hundred and one new permutations—"

"Are you my lover or my lawyer?" she asked.

He leaned back and stretched his long legs. "Both," he said with a lazy grin. "But you got the order right."

She smiled and blew her cigarette smoke away from

him, shooing it with her hand. "You make it so easy. Why is that?" she asked.

"Because I don't believe in guilt."

"Who does these days?"

"You. Paul. Everyone we know. It's the province of the privileged. It's expected among the upper middle class. Cultivated in the name of social consciousness."

She laughed because it was true. "Have you no social consciousness, then?"

"Social, sexual—I'm full of consciousness. But no guilt, I'm afraid."

"It's true, you know." She suddenly realized it. "You are the only person I know who isn't paralyzed by guilt. The lone nonneurotic left in our tax bracket."

She took another sip of wine and smiled at him. Then her face became pinched and serious again. "We have to tell her," she said. "About the separation, I mean. He won't. Paul will not tell her. He doesn't want to hurt her."

"He's a good man," Steve said.

"Pamela's a good woman."

Steven's blue eyes pinned her lazily. "My wife is good. Your husband is good. I am good and you are good. We are all good people."

Madeleine looked away from him. Then back. "Then why are we all so screwed up?"

"We?" Steve chuckled. It wasn't a malicious sound; he was simply amused, comfortable, contented.

Madeleine ground out her cigarette in the ashtray. "No. Not you, I guess. Come on, pal. Help me clear up this mess; the other one can wait one more day, I suppose. Then we've got to walk Shag."

He stood and kissed her lightly, accepted the two chili bowls she put in his hands, and carried them to

the counter near the dishwasher. When he returned
to the table she was standing there, staring off into
space, the bread basket in one hand, her wineglass
in the other.

"What's wrong now?" he asked gently.

"I love her, Steve. I love her, so I can understand
how he feels. I don't want to be without her. My
God," she said, "I'm feeling sorry for him. I'm feeling—"

"Guilty?"

"Yes. I guess. I love him, too, you know. Or I used
to. It's horrible to watch what this is doing to him.
What *he's* doing to himself. He's become like a—a little boy. He's afraid to leave home. That's what it is.
He's afraid to grow up and leave home."

"Finish your wine," Steven said. "It's a '55."

She drained the glass. "Aw," she said, "I'll give it
an 80."

They cleared the table and stacked the dishwasher
and left the chili pot to soak. Then Madeleine slipped
into her coat and rattled Shag's leash until the beast
bounded down from Franny's room where he'd been
mooning about all evening.

"Lonely, boy?"

Shag shook his head, yes, and his rump, no. Madeleine opened the door, handed Steve the pooper-
scooper, and slipped her arm through his. Shag was
already on his way to Central Park. The streets
seemed crisp and sweet after the rain. They walked
quietly. The dog, a few yards ahead, stopped to sniff
at hydrants and tree trunks and car tires.

"Shag," Madeleine called. "Come on, boy. Let's
cross."

"Where to?" Steve asked.

"Oh, Franny ran into some weirdo in the park today. It's given me the willies. Let's go over to Columbus Avenue."

They crossed at Seventy-sixth Street. Shag waited at the curb, then ran on ahead once Madeleine was safely over.

"Isn't there a law about keeping dogs on a leash?" Steve asked.

"He's perfectly trained. If there's one thing my hus—my almost ex-husband knows how to do, it's train a dog."

"This the last chore of the evening?"

"One more."

"That's not a chore," he balked.

Madeleine laughed. "I mean the garbage."

He kissed her. Then they looked up and Shag had disappeared.

"Shag—" Madeleine called tentatively.

"*Shag!*" Steve hollered.

In the distance, the lights of the Museum Café looked warm and cheery, and the dog bounded toward them, uncharacteristically passing up some of the finest old elms and fire hydrants in the neighborhood. The café was moderately crowded. It was just about the time of night when people would be wandering toward it for a late supper, and among them were Paul Philips and Carolyn Reid. In fact, they were just at the corner of Amsterdam Avenue, moseying up Seventy-seventh Street, each recalling the events of the evening from a different perspective.

The slender, blonde Juilliard grad student in the red angora beret was clutching Paul's arm and holding the program from the Metropolitan Opera House. Fresh to the wonders of New York, her first evening at the Met had left an irrepressible smile on her face; and a certain glow, seen on serious music students from out of town, inflamed her dewy cheeks.

"*Rosenkavalier* at the Met. I know it by heart, and now I've actually seen it—"

Paul was entrenched in his own comic opera of love and marriage, a melodrama to which an irritating new element had been added. "All I saw was a yellow Maserati," he said.

Still caught up with the production if *Rosenkavalier*, Carolyn shook her head. "I—I can't even make a value judgment—"

"That's it. Values. How do you teach them values? Maseratis at twelve!" He shook his head. "What's left? Mink at fourteen? Oh, I'm sorry. I said I wouldn't talk about it anymore. But—" He looked at her. "Look at you," he said. "Everything's exciting. Everything's new for you."

"When you live your whole life in Wisconsin, everything *is* new to you." She laughed.

Paul patted her hand and smiled. "Including married men who can't stop talking about their children?"

Her brow furrowed. "Curt was married," she said, "but he didn't have children. He always talked about his alcoholic wife."

Suddenly Carolyn's grip tightened on his arm. For a moment he thought it was the memory of Curt, whoever *he* was, that had set the poor kid trembling. Then he looked up to see a sheepdog galloping toward them.

"It's okay," he assured Carolyn, looking around for the dog's owner. "Why it looks just like—Shag—my daughter Franny's dog. Miniature sheepdog. Just about that size and color and—Shag?" he said, perplexed as the dog leaped happily at him. "It's okay. Down. Sit," he said firmly, brushing the paw prints from his trouser legs. "Uh—it is Shag," he told Carolyn who had let go of his arm and backed away.

Madeleine and Steve rounded the corner, and the sight of Shag attacking a stranger drew a cry from Madeleine. "Oh, my God—Shag!"

Steve, too, was concentrating on the dog. "Down, dog. Down. Heel!" he shouted. Then he looked up and stopped abruptly. "Paul—"

"Steve?"

Madeleine was steaming toward them. "Shag! Bad dog! Shag! I'm so sorry— He—" She stopped. "Paul," she said, switching abruptly from an apologetic tone to a scolding one.

"Madeleine," Paul said.

Steve's easy grin took in the pretty young blonde standing a little behind—but definitely with—Paul. "Madeleine said we had to walk the dog," he explained to both of them amiably.

"We were walking Shag—," Madeleine began.

Paul squared his shoulders and cleared his throat. "You ought to keep him on a lead."

Steve offered them the courtesy of distance by concentrating on the girl in the angora tam. "I'm Steven Sloan," he said, offering her his hand.

She shook it and smiled. "Carolyn Reid," she said.

He nodded at the program she was holding. "You've been to the opera."

"Remember my Aunt Charlotte?" Paul said suddenly, glancing from Madeleine to Carolyn to Steve and back. "Carolyn's a second cousin on her husband's side—once removed—"

"*Rosenkavalier*. It was wonderful," Carolyn told Steve.

"She's a graduate student at Juilliard. She's from Germantown," Paul blustered.

Madeleine's full lips were slightly parted. For want of anything better to do with them, she turned to the girl and made them form the word "Pennsylvania?"

"Wisconsin," said Paul quickly. "She's never been to the Met before."

"Have you ever been here before?" Steve asked, nodding toward the Museum Café.

"We were just going to have a bite to eat," Paul told Madeleine.

Carolyn, flushed partially because of the mad dog attack and partially because of her native enthusiasm, stared up at Steven Sloan with child-bright eyes. "I've never been to the Met before," she confided. "This is my fourth week in New York."

"Come on," Madeleine said to Shag.

"How do you like it?" Steve asked Carolyn.

"I missed dinner," Paul told Madeleine as she put the lead on the dog's collar and pulled at it. The dog wouldn't budge.

Madeleine tugged at the leash. "Shag!" she urged.

"New York?" Carolyn spread her arms and took a deep breath as if she would inhale and embrace the entire city. "I love it. I mean, something's always happening here."

Steve laughed.

"Shag!" Paul commanded. "Go with Madeleine."

He gave the dog a slap on the rump. With a whine of protest, Shag stood, shook himself, and prepared to move. Madeleine, agitated and eager to get away, practically dragged the mournful beast down the street.

Steven Sloan watched Madeleine's retreat. He started after her, then stopped. It would be impolite, if not uncool, to simply dash off, to run like a criminal from the innocent encounter.

"How's Pamela?" Paul asked him.

Steve smiled. "In the country. I have a client who's leaving for Europe tomorrow and a contract he has to sign—"

"Steve!" Madeleine called back, interrupting.

"Nice to meet you, Miss Reid."

"Thank you," Carolyn said.

Steve clapped Paul on the shoulder gently. "We'll get together—soon," he promised, and he moved off at a comfortable lope to catch up with Madeleine, who was waiting for him at the corner.

Paul watched them go.

"You didn't introduce me to the lady," Carolyn said.

"That was no lady. That was my wife." He shook his head and laughed at himself. "Oh, boy," he said.

"Oh, dear," said Carolyn.

"And my dog. And my friend." Paul stopped laughing.

Up the block and around the corner, Madeleine wasn't laughing either. She was walking briskly, seething silently. Steve walked quietly beside her. Only Shag's sudden infatuation for a particularly wide-based and mottle-barked tree slowed her pace.

"Angry?" Steve asked while Madeleine waited impatiently for Shag to sniff.

"I'm not angry," she said flatly. "I'm furious. Why am I furious?"

"Because he—," Steve suggested, pointing to Shag, "goes to him?"

"Because she's blonde and young, with no makeup and an eighteen-inch waist."

"What size shoe?"

"I'm the one who's been juggling a home and a job and a child and him and you," she said, ignoring his amusement. "I'm the one who's been sneaking around and guilty and up to my neck in *angst*—and he just shows up—there he is, with some blonde *fretzle*—! Don't laugh."

"I am not laughing."

"I am not jealous—"

"Good."

"God knows, all I want is out."

"Good."

"Why am I jealous?" she said miserably. He put his arm around her. "Oh, Steve—"

Shag finished and they walked on. "Look at the bright side," Steve suggested.

"Tell me about it."

He kissed her nose. "I know Paul," he said. "He'll tell Franny now."

Chapter Sixteen

They were in their pajamas, lying on the water
bed. At least Franny was lying on the bed. Jamie was
sitting cross-legged, staring at the giant screen of the
Advent television. Spread on the platform surrounding the sunken bed and floating on the quilted tide
was a forbidden feast: Cheez Doodles, cans of Coke,
and potato chips of every texture and taste. There
was also a bag of Famous Amos chocolate chips and
some less expensive, more mundane cookies, candies,
and crumbs.

Jamie was sucking on his braces, trying to dislodge
a tidbit of taco chip, but his eyes were wide and
glazed, fixed on Lon Chaney, Jr. in *The Mummy's
Curse*. He took a swig of Coke, sloshed the warm
syrupy liquid around his mouth, washed free the
taco crumb, and, without turning from the screen,
passed the can back to Franny. When she didn't take
it, he turned to look at her. Her head was buried
in the quilt.

"Hey." He thumped on the thick comforter. "Want
some Coke?"

"I can't look." The reply was muffled but earnest.

"Chicken."

The organ music that accompanied the movie was
intensifying, becoming high-pitched and weird.

"Tell me when I can look."

Jamie put down the Coke can and dipped back into the tangy pollen which was all that was left in the bag of puffed-up wormy-looking Cheez Doodles. He wet his finger, stuck it into the cheesy dust at the bottom of the cellophane bag, licked it, and, just as the mummy's hand crept out of the coffin, he shouted, "Now!" and Franny peeked at the screen.

"Nerd! Jerk! Cheater! Freak!" she screamed, and she clonked him over the head with a pillow. Jamie caught it and skittered away on his haunches, trying to keep his balance on the bouncing bed. He laughed and threw the pillow back at her.

"That was cruel, Jamie Harris. Cru-ell!"

"It's only—" He was laughing, crawling through the ebb and flow of scattered junk food. He felt his knee sink into the center of the Famous Amos bag and he felt the grinding crunch of cookies splintering beneath it. "Only a movie! Hey, cut it out!"

Franny lunged at him, caught his ankle, and began to tickle his toes. He tried to squirm away and succeeded, for a second, in loosening her grip on his foot, but she clamped onto the edge of his pajama leg, and he had to give up trying to pry open her hand because he had to keep his bottoms from sliding down. He clutched the elastic waistband frantically.

Franny quickly pressed her advantage. While Jamie tried to roll away, tugging at his bottoms and laughing and shouting, "Cut it. Hey, Franny. Look—the mummy! Look, look—he's gonna get you!" she let go of the pajama leg and scrambled up behind him to tickle his very vulnerable, very ticklish rib cage.

"Stop," he begged. "Stop!" But she wouldn't. They were both breathless, laughing and rolling on the rippling bed, crushing cookies and potato chips, crumb pellets shooting out from under them, spraying them, coating their hair and catching on the flannel of their pajamas.

She was quick, but he was stronger. Finally, he heaved himself up like the mummy itself and, with a great diverting roar, pinned her down. He straddled her, holding both her hands above her head, and, with one knee in the cookie crumbs and the other painfully lodged on a Coke can, he rode victoriously above her belly.

When she opened her eyes, Franny saw him laughing down at her. He was flushed and full of crumbs, and bits of chocolate chips freckled his pajama top and one of his cheeks. She laughed helplessly. Then she looked up to the mirror on the ceiling and she saw Jamie and herself coupled in a pose startlingly reminiscent of a drawing from *The Joy of Sex*.

The smile froze on her face. She turned pinker than the blushing tone of the illustration she'd recalled. "Let go," she said softly.

"Say I'm not cruel." His hands were like iron on her wrists. She squirmed uselessly, feeling confused, both annoyed at and proud of his unexpected strength.

"No."

He shook his head and showered her with cookie and potato chip crumbs. "Say you'll never tickle me again."

"No," she replied stubbornly. But he tightened his grip and she glanced again at their upside-down image in the mirror, and finally she said in a breathless burst, "You are not cruel and I will never tickle you again."

He let go and she tickled him. He grabbed her arms again immediately. "I had my toes crossed," she explained.

"Oh yeah. Oh sure," he said. She tried to wriggle out of his grasp again, and, again, she was stuck.

"Jamie—"

"What?" He had stopped laughing, too. His voice was strange—secretive and lower than usual.

"What do we do now?" she whispered.

The fact was he didn't know. He just hung on to her arms and stared down at her, and suddenly she went limp.

She stopped fighting and fell back onto the floating quilt. "I give up," she said, closing her eyes and pretending to swoon. "Kiss me. I'm yours," she whispered.

He laughed. Then he stopped laughing and considered the unexpected option. Then, awkwardly but very gently, he bent over and did kiss her, on the lips, once. She could feel his mouth curl into a pleased smile. Then he kissed her again. This time she made a little hurt noise, just a little surprised yelp, something between an *oh* and an *ouch.*

"What's the matter?"

She turned her head away. "Nothing," she said.

He let go of her arms. "Something's the matter."

She seemed deep in thought. "The book says—"

"What book?"

"The Joy of Sex."

Jamie nodded. "Yeah—" He'd read it, too. "It says anything's okay."

"If you like it," Franny reminded him.

"Don't you like it?"

He climbed off her and she rolled away, onto her side, and rested her head on her hand. "I like *you.*" She stared at him, appraising him unabashedly. "I like you better than Josh or Matthew or Andrew—"

"Andrew?" he groaned.

"But—"

"But what?"

"Nothing."

He knocked her hand out from under her chin. "Franny—"

"Your braces hurt!" she blurted at last.

"Oh, boy! Oh, wow! Oh, great." He moved away from her to a corner of the bed, sulking. It wasn't even a matter of the right technique or the right toothpaste. It was his braces! His braces!

"I'm sorry. You can't help it," she assured him. "It's not like it's your *fault*."

"No. Only I'll be sixteen or something before they come off."

She followed him to the corner of the bed and sat on her knees in front of him. He wouldn't look at her. Shyly, gently, she put her arms around him. He let her. He looked up. She closed her eyes and kissed him very, very softly on his full closed lips. "How long before you get a retainer?" she whispered when they parted.

Jamie climbed out of the bed pit and switched off the Advent. He grabbed the six-pack and some of the loose Coke cans. "Come on," he said, "we'd better get this junk out of here before Ralph comes back."

It took a little while to clear the food from the bed. They swept what crumbs they couldn't pick up into the space between the water bed and the platform around it, shook the quilt out over the Jacuzzi, and repaired the linens as best they could.

"Where do we sleep?" Franny asked.

"Shaggylon."

"With the birds and trees and plants—"

"And the piranhas."

They moved through the mirrored hallway, through the dining and meditation room, to the magical place. In one corner, stacked on the sweet-smelling straw tatami mats, were two cylinders that looked

like rolled reed knapsacks. Jamie took one and handed the other to Fran. "They're *futons*," he told her,
unrolling his beneath the shimmering skylight.

The unfurled futon looked like an exercise mat,
and Jamie opened a hidden closet and took out two
little Japanese headrests and two light but warm
quilts. Franny placed her futon a few feet from his,
and they lay down and snuggled under the quilts beneath the exotic greenery and the hanging baskets
and the wicker and white wrought-iron birdcages.
For some moments they lay flat on their backs, separate but warmly aware of one another, looking up at
the misted glass, listening to the rain.

"What happened?" Franny asked. "After they split,
I mean."

Jamie's hands were locked under his head. He
stared at the windswept clouds. "Ralph moved here.
And my mom sold our house."

Franny thought about her brownstone on Seventy-
fourth Street. She thought about the black lacquered
door and the flowers in the planter on the stoop and
her room with its velvet cushioned window seat and
her posters and the squeaky wicker headboard on
her bed. She felt her nose sting with tears.

"Was it a nice house?" she asked.

Jamie moved his mat a bit closer to hers. "It was
too big for the two of us. Is that headrest okay or do
you want a regular pillow?"

"It's okay."

They were silent for a while. Then Franny inched
her futon over toward Jamie's. "Jamie?" she whispered.

He grunted.

"You asleep?'"

"Yup." He rolled off his mat and pushed it nearer
to hers.

"What did they say?" she asked when he'd settled back under the quilt. "When they told you."

"I knew."

She stretched out her hands and felt the textured surface of the tatami on her palms. She took hold of her futon and sort of sidled it closer to Jamie's.

"They didn't just move out and sell a whole house and not tell you?"

"We went to McDonald's," he said.

"McDonald's?"

"They said we were going out to dinner and I could pick any restaurant I wanted to go to. I was nine. I picked McDonald's."

"I love McDonald's," Franny said. She turned onto her side and stared at him in the darkness. His eyes were closed.

"I had a Big Mac and french fries and a vanilla shake, and then they said that I knew they had problems—whew!" He smiled at the memory.

It wasn't a real smile. It was sort of lopsided; ironic, Franny thought. That was what they meant in books when they talked about an *ironic* smile.

"And they thought about it a lot and they decided that everybody would be a lot happier if Ralph moved out for a while."

He was silent. For a second it seemed as though he'd fallen asleep; then he opened his eyes and turned to face her. He propped his cheek on his arm. "Then they asked did I want a dog?"

"I've got a dog," she said morosely.

Jamie shook his head compassionately and moved his futon so that they were only inches away from one another. "Maybe you'll get ice skates."

"And then?" Franny found herself inching toward him, wriggling on the Japanese sleeping mat, under the cozy quilt, to the edge of her narrow futon and, unobtrusively, sliding her hand from under her quilt to under his. His side of the bed—because that's what it was now, not two futons, but one bed with two quilts—was warmer than hers.

"Then they say they love you." He moved his hand and it touched hers. He left it there, just their fingertips touching.

"And then?"

"I threw up. Listen," he said, "if they tell you to pick your favorite restaurant in the whole world, pick a restaurant you really hate. I haven't been able to eat a Big Mac since."

She thought about it a while. "I'll pick Chinese," she decided.

When Ralph returned an hour later, they were asleep. He reached for the light and then remembered that Jamie would be there. With his shoes in his hand, Ralph tiptoed over to the futons and looked down at the children.

The girl's thick dark hair was flowing over onto Jamie's sleeping pad, touching his son's sandy hair. In the soft night light their faces were smooth and sweet and carefree. Ralph smiled. His son was sleeping with a girl. They were sleeping innocently, but the sight was still strange—new and prophetic.

He stared at Jamie, and through the boy's face he could still see the baby's. It was there and it was gone, and it was an exciting and a sad thing to see. His son was growing up.

Book Three

Shaggylon

Chapter Seventeen

Steve Sloan's office, like the man himself, was handsome, impeccable, expensive-looking, and practically transparent. The wall of glass that looked onto a plushly carpeted corridor and the law library beyond it suggested a place and person with nothing to hide. Not a bad image for any lawyer to project, and better still for the youngest full partner of a prestigious five-name firm. The offices of Hausman, Ross, George, Young and Sloan were located on a high floor in a tall building at the corner of Madison Avenue and Fifty-seventh Street.

Madeleine had her back turned to the enormous conference table where she sat with Steve, Paul, and Paul's lawyer (a small, sharp, motherly looking wom-

an named Beatrice Baker). Madeleine was staring out
at the traffic heading uptown on Madison Avenue.
The cars, trucks, and buses surged forward like relay
runners whenever the synchronized traffic lights
turned green, and the taxis were weaving from lane
to lane with experienced stamina and an almost fierce
determination to lead the pack.

Madeleine was not in a winning mood. She felt as
small and angry as the yellow cabs looked, and, in
some ways, she felt as idiotically aggressive about
speeding along the one-way course on which she'd
embarked. There she was, Madeleine Strauss Philips
—heading uptown, careening from lane to lane to get
out front. Or was it just to get out first? To leave
Paul Philips panting in the dust? To win what?

"Insurance. The house. With all its contents—"
Steve checked off the items on his yellow legal pad.

"Not my stereo equipment," Paul said.

Madeleine turned back to the table. "He can have
all of it." A spark of annoyance fired her low voice.
"The tapes, the records. The *ear phones.*"

Why was she feeling so dull, so drained? Wasn't
she finally getting what she'd wanted—not the insurance or the house and its contents, but a divorce
from Paul? Freedom. She looked at him, and the
same feeling of loss that had made her turn toward
the window came over her again—the feeling that
the ride wasn't worth it, not for the meter price or the
tip.

She remembered, with a feeling of tiredness that
was also a memory, that she and Paul once had more
than what they were dividing up now. Franny had
Madeleine's dark hair and his blue eyes. And there'd
been another child who'd had Paul's sandy hair and
her dark eyes. Little Katie. Tiny, lost Kate. A dead
child: what once was, what might have been, what

was gone forever. A line from a poem by Dylan Thomas came to her: *After the first death, there is no other.*

"Child support to be divided equally," Paul's lawyer said.

Steve smiled affably. "That's stretching it, Bea."

"My client has been very generous—"

Steve tapped his pad with his pencil. "She has agreed to no alimony."

"She is a working woman," Bea reminded her colleague, returning his engaging smile.

"She works for the city. A new administration, she can be out on her ear."

Beatrice Baker was wearing a mauve cowl-necked sweater and a well-tailored no-nonsense suit. She glanced pleasantly at Madeleine, briefly studying the younger woman's tense but attractive face, her clothing—simple, stylish, very Bloomingdale's—her sensible but expensive watch. Even the makeup Madeleine had applied so artfully was barely discernible, but, Bea was willing to bet, was department store priced and purchased and worn over a couple of hundred dollars' worth of Klinger or Lazlo cleansing, toning, and moisturizing products.

Bea smiled benevolently. "She's worked steadily for years. She earns a sizable income—"

"And as a single mother," Steve said, "she'll pay sizable taxes."

"I'll pay one-fourth of the child support," Madeleine volunteered suddenly.

"We accept." Without glancing at Paul, Beatrice quickly jotted down the altered figure.

"Madeleine—" Steven raised an eyebrow at her. He didn't raise it very high, just enough to suggest that she please keep her pretty mouth shut and let him negotiate on her behalf.

"It's fair," she protested to him. "His income is four times mine."

"If you don't count what your father left you," Paul said sourly.

"Custody," Steve announced. "We now come to custody—" He paused dramatically, then tapped his pad with the end of his pencil. He looked each of them squarely in the eye—kindly, compassionately— first Madeleine, then Paul. "I've known you both a long time," he began. "I know you love Franny and I know you want to do what's best for her."

Paul glanced at Beatrice. Without acknowledging his glance, she announced, "My client wants full custody."

"Alternate weekends," said Steve. "Alternate vacations; one month in the summer."

Bea nodded understandingly and smiled. "He is *not* going to be a weekend father."

"Every-*other*-weekend father," Madeleine corrected her.

"No way!" said Paul.

"Sue me!" said Madeleine.

"All the way to the Supreme Court!"

"Try to prove I'm an unfit mother—!"

Steve ran his long manicured fingers through his thick dark hair. Then he tapped a muffled tattoo with his eraser tip on the white marble conference table. "Okay, simmer down—cool it—"

Without too much conviction, Bea added, "Perhaps a marriage counselor—might help."

She seemed almost prepared for Paul and Madeleine's immediate and simultaneous "No!"

Bea closed her eyes, opened them to look at Steven Sloan who shrugged the ball back into her court, then turned to them again. "What does your daughter have to say?" she asked innocently.

"Say?" Madeleine stormed. "He won't tell her!"

"Paul," Steve said gently, "you've got to tell her."

"I said I'd tell her when this was settled—"

"How can it be settled?" Flinging her arms open, Madeleine addressed her question to God, the ceiling, or, perhaps, Peecher and Sidel, the advertising agency on the floor above.

"I think—" Beatrice smiled encouragingly at Paul, "you both have to talk to her."

Steven agreed.

"May I make a suggestion?" Bea reached out as if to pat both parents' hands, but she withdrew her own gracefully to form a judicious, prayerful clasp. "These things are difficult at best, but you can make it a little easier on yourselves. You're both very emotional—"

Perhaps that was why she'd clasped her hands, Madeleine thought. Perhaps she'd had enough experience with tug-of-war parents to know what danger lurked in a comforting touch. Madeleine lit a cigarette and glanced out at the traffic again. She seriously wondered whether, if she hadn't had the filter stub to gnash, she might have flung herself across the table and sunk her canines into the dignified, composed, comforting lady lawyer Paul had got himself. She figured the chances at fifty-fifty.

"Letting go, in front of her," Bea was saying, "well, that imposes an extra burden. Plan something. Take her someplace she likes—"

Chapter Eighteen

"When did you decide you like Chinese food?" Paul asked Franny.

The three of them were sitting at a large round table in the restaurant Jamie said Ralph had suggested when he'd asked him about a Chinese place far enough away from West Seventy-fourth Street so that Franny wouldn't have to pass it and think about it every day. Of course Jamie hadn't told Ralph why he needed such information. Not the real reason anyway. He'd sort of hinted that he might be wanting to go to an out-of-the-way place himself; he sort of said, "You know, like if, maybe, I might just want to take someone someplace where I wouldn't have to, like, run into, you know, *people*—"

Ralph must have smiled his broadest capped-teeth smile, and—since he couldn't wink and poke Jamie in the ribs because the conversation had taken place on the telephone—Jamie could *hear* Ralph smile. Ralph seemed absolutely delighted to research just the right place, and he'd come up with an out-of-the-way but superb, attractive, fairly expensive— but not to worry, he'd told Jamie, because he had a credit line there which the maître d' would gladly extend, on a moment's notice, to his son, just let him know when—Chinese place called King Dragon.

The day Paul and Madeleine had asked her to choose her favorite restaurant in the whole world,

Franny's heart fell through her stomach. She felt the sweat beads breaking out on her forehead, wiped them away with the back of her hand as if she were pushing her hair back, and smiled so hard it actually hurt. If she hadn't smiled and kept her eyes very wide open, she'd have cried and blown the whole thing. "Can I think about it?" she'd asked.

"Of course, honey."

"Friday night. We'll go this Friday, okay Paul?"

"I was thinking of Sunday. I—"

"Saturday," said Madeleine.

"Sunday—sure you can think about it, honey," he told Franny.

She'd held the smile one minute more, then turned and walked swiftly from the room.

"And where'd you ever hear about this place?" Paul continued as the waiter placed Madeleine's white wine and Paul's scotch before them. There were tea-cups on the white linen tablecloth and a teapot and a bowl of crisp noodles. Franny sat with her hands folded in her lap.

"She said one of the kids from school recommended it," Madeleine reminded Paul, "and her liking Chinese food—it's a sign she's growing up."

"I didn't ask—" *You*, was what he was going to say. He restrained himself. "You're the prettiest girl here," he told Franny, "and you certainly are growing up fast." The last part sounded more like an accusation than a compliment in spite of his proud paternal smile. The accusation aspect entered as the smile left and he stared pointedly at Madeleine.

The waiter put an order to Mu Shu pork on the table. The pork, egg, and vegetable mixture in one steaming bowl and the rice-flour pancakes, plum sauce, and shredded scallions in separate bowls.

"You have to try everything in this world," Madeleine said, a bit more aggressively than she'd intended. Then she looked away from Paul and stroked Franny's hair. "If you don't try it, Franny, how do you know you don't like it?"

Like divorce? Paul wanted to ask. Here, Franny, eat a little marriage. Don't like it? Try divorce. He stared at the bowl of Mu Shu pork. It looked the way he felt: a chopped, diced, sliced, and failed experiment. And Madeleine was the Cuisinart.

"She's tried Chinese food since she was three, and she's always hated it," he said. "Are you sure you don't want a Coke, honey?"

Madeleine put a pancake on Franny's plate and one on her own. "Now, first you take a pancake and this plum sauce. It's good."

"You can have a Coke if you want one," Paul said a little louder.

"You start by putting the sauce on the pancake, and then you add the filling." Madeleine spooned a bit of the pork mixture onto Franny's pancake, then plucked up a few scallions with her fingers and started to sprinkle them onto the pork, egg, and vegetables.

"If you don't like scallions, you can leave out the scallions," Paul said. He took a solid slug of scotch.

"She loves scallions."

"Since when?"

Madeleine ignored the question. "Then you fold it up and—it's like a taco. See. You can eat it with your fingers."

"You can use a fork if you want to."

"Do you want to taste the inside first?"

"Do you want to try chopsticks?"

"Paul—" Madeleine said, exasperated.

He drank again, sullenly. "I was just asking."

"Taste it, honey," Madeleine urged.

"Try it, Franny."

Franny, using a fork, took a small bite of the food and swallowed it. Madeleine seemed relieved. She reached for her wine. Paul sipped his scotch again.

"You're going to get a divorce, right?" Franny said.

The scotch stopped high in Paul's gullet and began to back up. Madeleine's face froze and her fingers strangled the stem of her wineglass.

"Fran—" Paul gurgled before the coughing fit overtook him.

"Franny—" Madeleine released the glass before the stem snapped.

Franny seemed not to notice their distress. She picked at her food and then continued in a practical and distant tone, "It's okay. I mean, it's all for the best, isn't it? You won't have to pretend anymore—that you're happy when you're not. Anyway, half of everybody I know's parents are divorced, and it's not so terrible. It's not like cancer or being dead or something—"

She chewed solemnly, swallowed hard, and turned to Madeleine. "You won't have to say daddy's working late when he's not home for dinner—" She looked at Paul. "And you won't have to wake me up in the morning when you're not even sleeping in our house—"

He couldn't bear her calmness—or the look in her eyes that betrayed it. "You told her—," he hissed at Madeleine. "You promised you wouldn't tell her."

But Madeleine's mouth was opened wordlessly and her eyes were as hurt as Franny's. "I—I didn't. I swear it," she said.

Franny cut them both off. "You won't argue anymore either," she reminded them. "And time flies, doesn't it? You always say that. Because after this

year, there's only junior high and high school, and
then I'll be in college and you won't have to worry
about me because I'll be gone, too."

She was trying to sound so grown-up. *She* was trying to comfort and protect *them*. It was easy enough
to see the pain beneath her candor and almost impossible to think of a way to relieve it. Their child
had become a compassionate parent and they two
stunned and helpless human beings.

"Franny—" It was all Paul could say.

Madeleine reached for her daughter's hand. It was
clammy cold. She held it, rubbed it softly, soothingly
between her own.

Franny smiled weakly. "I—I know you both love
me," she said. "And I don't need new ice skates."
She pushed her chair back from the table and stood
up.

"Ice skates?" Paul said.

"Where are you going?" Madeleine asked.

"I'm going to throw up now," Franny told her.

Paul paid the check while she was gone. He
couldn't think of anything to say to Madeleine. He
thought about holding her hand. She was pale, almost green. He thought he'd like to make her feel
better, but he had this pounding headache all of a
sudden. Maybe it was the MSG. They said Chinese
food had loads of monosodium glutamate in it and
that it gave quite a few people headaches.

He rubbed his temples and stared down at Madeleine's hand, which lay exactly where Franny had
left it when she'd slipped her own icy little hand out
from under it.

"I—I'd like to come home tonight," he said.

Madeleine shook her head. "Not tonight, Paul.
Give me my moment with her tonight—"

"Okay. I'll pick her up tomorrow morning. Outside.

When she's ready for school. But tell her that you wanted to be alone with her tonight—please."

"Yes. I will."

"That it wasn't my idea—I mean about tonight."

"All right," Madeleine said.

The cab dropped them off at Seventy-fourth Street. They had decided that Madeleine and Franny would get out there and Paul would keep the cab and head downtown to the apartment on West Sixty-ninth. But when they finally stopped in front of the brownstone, he got out and paid the driver.

"I'll walk," he assured Madeleine. "I need the air." He stood awkwardly for a moment looking up at the house. Then he bent to hug Franny and kiss her good night. He hugged her tightly but the kiss was soft; the kisses, really. One on each cheek and one against her temple, brushing her thick hair lightly, lovingly. "It'll be okay, pumpkin," he promised.

She was trying not to cry. She whispered something against his ear. He didn't understand it immediately, couldn't quite hear it. Then he knew. "Who's going to water the milk? Who's going to butter the cream?" she'd whispered. Then she turned and ran up the steps. Madeleine rushed after her.

Paul waited until they were both inside, the black door latched, the hall light on. Then he took off his glasses, put them into his breast pocket, put up his jacket collar, and walked away in the greenish glow of the mugger-proof streetlights.

Franny ran straight up the inside stairs. She ran into her room and shut the door and changed into her old flannel pajamas and jumped into bed. She'd even switched off the light and was lying in the darkness when Madeleine came to tuck her in. Franny said nothing when her mother sat down on the edge of her bed and turned the light back on. Her eyes

were wide open, glazed with tears. She was staring at
the ceiling, facing Madeleine but not looking at her.

Madeleine stroked her forehead and cheeks. She
straightened the little pink collar of Franny's pajama shirt and smoothed the shoulders and started to
button a button that was missing. "Have to fix that,"
she mumbled. Then she saw how tight the pajamas
had become. She noticed the outline of her daughter's
budding nipples and the beginning swell of her
breasts. She smiled. "You're beginning to develop,"
she said warmly.

Franny pulled the covers up to her neck. "No, I'm
not."

A shiver of hurt threatened Madeleine's smile. "Do
you want to sleep with me tonight, Bubbs?" she asked
softly.

Franny didn't answer.

"I'll leave the door open. In case you want anything."

She bent to kiss her, but Franny turned her face
away. Madeleine ran the back of her hand over
Franny's cheek and forehead, smoothing, soothing,
gently stroking her daughter's head as she spoke.

"You want to hit me? Or yell? Why not? You're
right." Her husky voice was deeper than usual, and
slightly tremulous. "I don't know how to explain it
except it's not you, Franny—it's daddy and me. When
I married daddy, I was twenty years old and I
thought I knew everything. Then—do you remember after little Katie died? No, you were too little."

Madeleine shook her head and smiled sadly, but
Franny only continued to stare, to keep her teeth
clenched and lips shut, making her soft childish jaw-
line rigid and sharply defined. Madeleine reached to
touch the odd unforgiving jaw, then withdrew her
hand.

"I made a nest," she continued. "Daddy and me and Franny made three. I wouldn't leave it. Someday, when you grow up, you'll understand. But, finally, I had to grow up and get out. I changed, Franny. I'm still changing. And daddy doesn't want anything to change."

Franny closed her eyes and put her hands over her ears. Madeleine pulled her hands down and held onto the child's slender wrists. "I love you, Franny. I love you, and we have each other, and I'm never going to give you up!"

The tears came then, finally, the cleansing, angry, helpless tears. Madeleine lifted her gently, held Franny tight in her arms, rocking her, comforting her. "It's all right. Everything's going to be all right. I promise," she said almost defiantly. "I promise you, Franny. And you know I never break a promise. You'll see, baby. You'll see."

Gradually Franny's sobbing subsided. Madeleine kissed her and wrapped her in her comforter. Quietly, she turned off the light.

"Did you love each other," Franny asked in the darkness, "when you made me?"

"We did, Franny. We really, truly did—"

Chapter Nineteen

The next morning, as Franny was leaving for school, she saw a strange woman with a slip of paper in her hand coming toward the house. The woman appeared to be checking the house numbers as she moved toward the Philips's brownstone. Franny hurried down the steps, unaware of her father waiting across the street until he shouted her name. She glanced at him and waved, then rushed up to the older woman.

"It's not for sale," she said breathlessly. "The house—"

The woman blinked at her and said something in Spanish.

"This house," Franny said slowly. "It's not for sale. Not for sale!"

The woman shook her head and moved on down the street, still checking the address on the piece of paper against the house numbers of the buildings on the block.

As Franny watched her apprehensively, Paul came across the street. "Hi." He kissed her. "I'll get Shag and walk you to school."

"I walked him already," she said. The woman entered a building near the corner. "It's all right," Franny told Paul before he could protest. "Shag went."

"Did you water the milk and scratch the chickens?"

Franny stared at him as if he were speaking a

116

foreign language. The game was over. "You don't have to walk him anymore," she said.

They continued toward the corner in silence.

"How did you know I wasn't sleeping at home?" Paul asked at last.

"I saw you. Every day."

He started to say something. Then changed his mind. After a bit, he said, "Then you pretended, too. That you were sleeping. Every day."

Franny stopped. "I don't want you to walk me to school anymore. I'm not a baby. I'm twelve years old and I can walk by myself now."

She started off without him, but he stopped her. "Your mother and I have our problems, but we're going to work them out. It's going to be all right," he said urgently. "You'll see, Franny. You'll see. I love you and you're going to come and live with me and—"

"I'm only twelve years old!" she screamed. She tore herself free of him, clamped her hands over her ears, and ran away. His eyes filled with tears as he watched her go, but he made no move to stop or follow her.

She was still running when Elliot Freeman spotted her from the bus. He was standing next to Jamie, carrying a copy of the Racing Form and describing his system for picking sure winners. "So far, I'm ahead forty-two dollars for the month," Elliot said, crashing against a gangly boy with a bulky leather dance bag slung over his shoulder.

"Well excuse *me*," the boy said when Elliot failed to either acknowledge or apologize for the collision. The bus was crowded with kids on their way to school as well as working people, elderly shoppers, and the early-bird shift of unemployment compensation collectors.

Jamie whistled in admiration. "Forty-two dollars—"

"Less ten percent which my crummy brother takes for placing the bets," Elliot grumbled.

"That's usury."

"It's the pits." That was when he glanced out the window and saw her. "See Franny run—" He said it as though he were reciting from a Dick and Jane primer.

Jamie ducked and peered past Elliot and the dance bag boy. Even at a distance he could tell that something was wrong, and he pulled the cord for the bus to stop.

"Hey," Elliot called as Jamie pushed his way to the rear door. "Hey, it's the wrong stop, stupid." But Jamie had jumped out and was racing after Franny Philips.

He caught up with her at the corner of Seventy-sixth Street just as she was about to run across against the light. He grabbed her brown fringed jacket to stop her. "What's going on?"

She spun on him. "Go away!"

The light said DON'T WALK, but there was a break in the traffic and Franny dashed across the street. Jamie followed her. "Franny! Will you stop?" He was running to catch up with her. "Come on. Stop!" But she didn't answer or stop until the light and the traffic forced her to a halt. "Will you tell me what's the matter?" he said, slowing beside her.

"Nothing!" She held her sides and breathed hard. "I hate them," she said finally.

Jamie only nodded. When the light changed, he walked across the street with her. At the corner of Seventy-ninth Street she abruptly turned left, toward Riverside Park. Jamie followed her. "Where are you going?"

At first she seemed not to hear him, then she

shrugged. He looked up at the sound of rock and roll music coming toward them. Two teen-aged boys were heading aimlessly down a park path. One had a huge transistor tape deck/radio strapped over his shoulder, and the other was whacking at the bushes with a broken tree branch. Instinctively, Jamie took Franny's arm and steered her past them down toward the boat basin plaza.

"You run away and they find you and then they send you to a shrink," Jamie said as they walked along the roadway overlooking the water's edge.

"How do you know?"

He didn't answer. He just let go of her arm. But she looked at him and remembered that he was speaking from experience again. "Oh," she said.

"It's not like the pediatrician," he reassured her. "You don't get any shots."

They walked on for a while in silence, watching the marina, the boats, the morning joggers. A drunk carrying a bottle in a paper bag weaved unsteadily along the path. An expensively outfitted middle-aged runner trotted by, barely grazing him, and the bottle slipped. The bleary-eyed drunk recovered it, mumbled something, and reached out for a tree. He knocked wood and took a hearty gulp from the bottle.

"Like—they're the ones who really need help," Jamie said.

At first Franny thought he meant the poor old drunk leaning against the tree, but then she realized that he was talking about their parents.

"What kind of help?"

"Shrink help."

They walked down the steps toward the marina.

"Did yours go?" Franny asked.

"How do you think my mother met Simon?"

"No kidding—"

They walked to the chain link fence that cordoned off the marina from the rest of the park, and they stood there, pressed against the fence, looking out at the boats beyond. Some were elaborate houseboats; more were smaller, jauntier-looking crafts; and there were a few handsome sailboats bobbing on the white-capped waters of the Hudson River. Jamie looked at the boats and then looked north to the Palisades and south where the Statue of Liberty guarded the channel to the sea and a freedom too vast to contemplate.

"If I'd gone to sailing camp instead of tennis camp—," Jamie said.

What if? We'd sail away was what he'd meant. Sure. In a million years maybe.

Franny pushed against the marina gate. It was locked. "Where can we go?" She said it so softly he'd hardly heard her, but his thought was the same.

"Listen. I've got this key—"

Franny looked at him and waited.

"And—" Jamie pulled out his wallet, practical as ever. "A bus pass."

"Shaggylon?" she whispered.

He tried not to smile. He took her hand and they ran out of the park to the crosstown bus stop.

In the morning traffic it took them nearly half an hour to get from Seventy-ninth and Broadway to Ralph's apartment in the East Sixties. They left their shoes under the little oriental table in the mirrored hallway and tiptoed into the incredible jungle. It was, if possible, even more beautiful by the light of day. Slivers of dusty sunbeams streamed through the magical forest. The birds were active, cawing and singing. The glass ceiling created little rainbows in odd corners, and the soothing, fragile tatami mats that covered the floors were warm with sunlight.

"What are we going to do?"

Jamie waggled his eyebrows like Groucho Marx. "Wanna play doctor?"

Franny blushed.

"No, seriously. Look, you just lay down there—"

"Where—on the floor?"

"Unroll a futon."

"I want to go now."

"Franny—I mean shrink doctor. Come on, you ran away, didn't you? I'll be your psychiatrist now."

He unrolled a futon for her and she lay back on it rather melodramatically, like a dead Egyptian princess, her arms folded across her chest. Jamie groaned. "We're not playing *Return of the Mummy's Curse.* You're supposed to be a patient. Now just relax and tell me—" He settled himself cross-legged behind her. "What did you dream last night?"

"I never dream."

"Everybody dreams. It's a scientific fact."

"I had a dream, but I didn't have it last night," she said cautiously. When Jamie waited in silence, she continued. "I'm walking Shag," she said, closing her eyes, "and it's dark out. We start crossing the street and then—it opens. The street just opens and I fall. Shag barks, but nobody hears him, and I keep falling. I can't stop falling and I'm going to land and die and then—" She opened her eyes and turned to look at him and changed her mind and shut her eyes tightly again. "And then I wake up."

Jamie waited. He thought about it. "That means something. No, don't get up yet," he cautioned her, still trying to puzzle out the symbolism of the dream. "Only I don't know what it means," he capitulated at last. "Let's try something else. Say the first thing that comes into your head."

"You're not a very good shrink."

"Oh, great—"

"I'm sorry. That's what came into my head."

The telephone rang. Franny gasped and sat up. Jamie grabbed her wrist. "The phone," he told her, loosening his grip a little but not letting go.

"Ssshh—" she cautioned, staring in the direction of the ringing telephone.

"They can't hear us," Jamie whispered.

"They found us—" Franny was whispering too, "and we're going to get into such trouble—"

"They can't find us. School thinks we're home and home thinks we're at school, and Ralph's off on a shoot and—" He cleared his throat and said out loud, "Why are we whispering?"

The phone stopped ringing.

"What if he just comes back?"

"Ralph? He's in New Mexico shooting sky divers. Relax."

Her shoulders slumped forlornly. "I can't."

"You're really neurotic," Jamie said, annoyed.

She smiled then. "That's why I have a shrink."

"Okay." He laughed. "Your hour is up, Miss Philips. That will be seventy-five dollars, please." He stood and held out his hand for the payment. Franny took his hand and heaved herself up.

"Is that what it costs?" she asked, awed. He had started for the kitchen. She followed him.

"That's what Simon gets."

Jamie went directly to the refrigerator and opened it. The choice was limited: a bottle of champagne, three Heineken beers, a jar of olives, and some left-over pâté.

"Seventy-five dollars an hour?" Franny whistled. "Your mother sure saved a lot when she married him."

"Yeah. But she got Melody. You want a beer?"

"I hate beer. Who's Melody?"

Jamie pulled out the champagne. "Melody's Simon's daughter. My stepsister. Hah! When you've got Melody, you really need Simon."

Jamie was trying to open the champagne. He'd succeeded in shaking it up pretty well, but the cork hadn't budged.

"I don't think this is such a good idea—" Franny said.

"Hold the bottom," he told her. She held the bottom of the bottle with two hands while Jamie stripped away the blue and silver foil and unwound the wire that fastened the cork to the neck of the bottle. She still didn't think it was such a good idea.

"He'll know it's gone."

"Ralph never remembers anything. Except my birthday," he assured her. And suddenly the cork popped, and the champagne exploded from the bottle like a bubbly fountain in a child's playground. It shot straight up, then cascaded in umbrella arcs around them. Jamie leaned his head back and opened his mouth wide to catch some of the wine. Franny laughed and wiped her wet face with her hands and then licked the sour-sweet liquid from her fingers.

They tidied the kitchen haphazardly, blotting up the spill with paper towels and napkins and, finally, one of the huge fluffy bath towels that hung beside the Jacuzzi, over Ralph's heated neon towel rack. Then they took the champagne bottle into the living room and passed it back and forth as they sat on the unfurled futon beneath the snake tree under the glass greenhouse roof.

Franny sipped daintily and handed the bottle back to Jamie. "Do you know what I want to do?" she said lazily.

"What?"

"I want to stay right here. Forever." She sighed and took the bottle back from him and drank again.

He watched her, and he frowned thoughtfully. Then he smiled. "We can't stay here forever." He let her pour champagne into his mouth, held up his hand when he'd had enough, and swilled the liquid between his cheeks. It felt a little like a Water Pik bubbling against his braces. "But if you want," he continued, "if you want to, we can stay here this weekend."

Chapter Twenty

"Ma—"

Franny stood, hairbrush in hand, staring down at her mother's blanket-covered body. Madeleine's fists were clutching the pillow so hard that her knuckles were white, and her eyes were clenched almost as tightly as her jaw. She was sleeping hard.

Fran glanced at the Braque lithographs on the brick wall over the bed. There were two of them, both in shades of blue and gray. She'd always thought they were pictures of birds, the top one flying east, the bottom west—two things headed in opposite directions. Like her mother and father, she thought. She wondered if the birds had made their way into Madeleine's dreams.

"Ma, it's time." She shook her mother gently.

Numb, still asleep, Madeleine automatically sat up, took the hairbrush, and set to work on Franny's hair. She parted it down the middle and gave Franny half to hold as she brushed and began to braid the other half.

Franny stared at the dressing table, the desk, the bookshelf wall of the bedroom, away from Madeleine's puffy half-lids. She took a little breath; then she plunged in.

"Jamie's mom has a country house, and they want me to go with them for the weekend."

"Weekend?" Madeleine rasped in her husky morning voice.

Franny lifted her hand. Madeleine nodded blindly toward it, and her head almost toppled with the effort. She waited, squinted, reached for the elastic band on Franny's wrist, and fastened the braid.

"They'll pick us up Friday, right after school," Franny said quickly.

Madeleine started on the second braid. Slowly. "School—" she mumbled. "School—something—Ahh," she said. "Saturday. Art school."

"Once. I'll just miss it once. Oh, mom, it's the country. Do you know how long it's been since I've had some fresh air?"

"I have to ask your father—" Finished with the hair, she fell back onto the pillows.

"No you don't," Franny said almost angrily.

She tugged at her braids, as if that tiny hurt could take the place of the sadness that had caused her sudden anger at her father and her mother. She tugged at her braids as if she were testing their tightness, and when she faced Madeleine again, her face was as emotionless as Jamie would have wanted it to be.

"You don't have to ask him anymore."

Madeleine opened her eyes. "Oh," she said, reaching for her cigarette pack.

Franny kissed her cheek. "Thanks, ma. That's neat," she said as she ran from the room.

She wanted to phone Jamie, but she had to walk Shag. She ran the dog around the block twice, then slowed to let him sniff at his favorite hydrant. It's done, she kept thinking. She would have her weekend in Shaggylon. A weekend away from grown-ups, a weekend to forget about what was happening—and not to think or feel too much about what would happen next.

"Good dog, Shaggy. Good, wonderful Shag!" He wagged his tail, delighted with the unexpected run and the compliment. Franny deftly tidied up behind him and dropped the little green bag into a nearby garbage can.

As they approached the house, she saw her father waiting on the other side of the street. He seemed apprehensive, as if he didn't quite know whether he should smile at her or not. She waved to him, and he appeared puzzled, but he grinned gratefully and hurried across to her.

"I—I'm not walking you to school—" he began.

She smiled and kissed his cheek. "Let me take Shag in and get my books. I'll be right back."

He smiled weakly, surprised. "You want me to wait for you?"

"Sure."

It wasn't until she was putting her knapsack over her suede jacket that she remembered how angry at him she had been yesterday. She wondered briefly if that was why he was acting so oddly today. It was too bad she couldn't tell him why she was so happy this morning.

"Hi," she called, coming down the steps toward him.

He was still on good behavior. "I didn't come here to walk you to school," he reassured her. "I know you're a big girl now. I'm just walking you to the corner—okay?"

She slipped her arm through his. "I'll walk you to the corner," she said.

He patted her hand and held it. "Are you all right?"

They were at the corner. "Sure." She stood on her

toes and hugged and kissed him, then ran across the street and waved good-bye.

He waved back and watched, puzzled, as she practically skipped off to school. She's all right, he thought to himself. Without realizing it, he smiled with delight. At least, he thought, Franny's all right again.

At his office, he waited until 10:30, then he phoned Madeleine.

"She's all right, Maddy," he said when she picked up. "I mean, she's herself again."

Madeleine sighed. "Thank God," she murmured. "I think she just had to get it all out of her system."

"We're very lucky."

She could hear the pride in his voice, and the love. "I know. Paul?"

It was just a moment, a moment when she almost asked whether she should let Franny spend the weekend with the Peterfreunds, a moment when she wanted to share his pride and love of their daughter with him again, a moment when everything that had seemed so right and clear before he'd called seemed suddenly muddy. And then the moment passed.

"Thanks for calling," she said gently.

By the time her parents finished their conversation, Franny was wriggling uncomfortably on her seat, stuck between Susan Metzger and Elliot Freeman in the informal semicircle around Mr. Ricci. What a terrific way to spoil a terrific day, she was thinking.

It wasn't bad enough that she'd gotten trapped between the wimp and the goon, but she was facing the blackboard (which was green), and on it one sentence among several stared accusingly back at her: *What is a lie?*

Franny glanced over at Jamie, seeking solace from her partner in crime. He wasn't looking at her. He was watching Mr. Ricci, who taught what the curriculum sheet described as "Ethics— A class dealing in basic moral choices." Mr. Ricci was young, bearded, and enthusiastic.

"Okay," he said, moving on to *What is stealing?*, "you take money out of someone's locker, that's clearcut. That's stealing. Now, let's take this situation—"

"Ethics is so bor-ing," Susan whined to Franny.

"You are so bor-ing," Franny whispered.

Undaunted, Susan continued. "I wish it was vacation—"

Franny glanced at Jamie once more, then followed his eyes back to Mr. Ricci.

"Say your mother sent you to the supermarket, and the groceries add up to seven and a half dollars—"

"Are you kidding?" one of the boys called out.

Mr. Ricci ignored him. "And you give the check-out person a ten-dollar bill, and instead of giving you back—"

"Two and a half bucks—" Elliot computed quickly.

"One of the dollar bills," said Mr. Ricci, "is a ten. Now, what do you do about the extra ten dollars?"

"Keep it," Elliot shouted.

"You can't keep it." Susan sounded almost angry. "It's not yours."

"So what?" Martha Rockwell asked.

"You've got to give it back."

Jesse Poppick said, "Are you nuts?"

"Okay. Hold it. Keep it down." Mr. Ricci smiled benevolently. "Say you do keep it. After all, it was the check-out person's responsibility, right? Have you stolen the ten dollars?" He was looking at Franny.

"It's the same as stealing, but it's not stealing," she began.

"Why not?" Mr. Ricci grinned and nodded encouragingly.

Suddenly Franny wasn't quite sure why not.

Jamie saw her momentary confusion. "Because you didn't go out to rip them off in the first place," he said, coming to her rescue.

"That's right. It just happened," she told Mr. Ricci.

"Right," he said. "It just happened. But you still have a choice. So what choice do you make?"

Melissa Middleberg, a shy, angelic-looking girl, raised her hand. "Mr. Ricci? Mr. Ricci?"

"Yes, Melissa."

"This happened to me," the girl said. "I was visiting my grandmother in Florida and this exact same thing happened. At a supermarket. We were walking out the door when my grandmother noticed."

Mr. Ricci was already nodding and smiling. "And what did your grandmother say, Melissa?"

The girl looked down at her hands folded in her lap. "She said, 'Let's get the hell out of here.'"

The class exploded with laughter. Even Mr. Ricci laughed. Melissa turned red and just smiled a little. Then the bell rang and the joke was carried out into the hall by the rambunctious students. They were still talking about it after school.

"Did your grandmother actually say that?" Susan pumped the shy Melissa, who nodded again and giggled.

"Don't tell—"

"Don't tell?" Elliot said. "You're asking Susan Metzger not to tell?"

Susan turned her red nose up at Elliot and her attention to Jamie. "Are you going to the party?" she asked him. "There's going to be a live group. I know the Collegiate boys are going to crash."

Jamie looked at Franny. "I'm going to East Hampton," he said.

"I'm going to—" Franny was stuck. She couldn't be going to the same place.

"Westport?" asked Jamie.

"Westport," she said. "See you, Susan."

Franny and Jamie walked away from the group gathered on the school steps.

"They're in love," Susan confided to Melissa.

"How do you know?"

"I've got antennae. My father says."

They crossed West End Avenue together, then said good-bye at the corner and each walked separately toward home; Franny turned right, Jamie left. Two blocks apart, they headed for Riverside Park and met on the way to the boat basin. They walked along in silence, back to the fence that had kept them out of the marina. The gate was still locked.

Jamie leaned his back against the fence. Franny held onto it, pressing her forehead against the cool metal. They had come to make plans, but there didn't seem to be anything to say.

"I'm glad."

"Me, too."

"I wish it was tomorrow." Franny said, staring out at the boats.

"I wish it was today."

Me, too, she thought several hours later. She was in her room, sitting in her desk chair under her table-model hair dryer. It was a bright orange plastic thing decorated like a Martian's helmet with two small antennae on top that vibrated with the electrical current.

The Joy of Sex rested in her lap, opened to the back pages which had become her diary. I wish it was today, she thought, but she didn't write it down. Her pen was poised above the page. She reread the last entry:

October 15. | DIVORCE |

She stared at the ugly word boxed in black ink. Finally, she wrote beneath it: October 20, October 21. And in red ink, she wrote and underlined the word *Shaggylon*.

She ruffled through the pages of the book before closing it. One of the illustrations caught her eye. She reached back and set the book down on her desk. Then she pressed her hands against the sides of her breasts, trying to get them to look something like the woman in the book. She looked down at herself, searched for a sign of cleavage, and sighed.

No way. There was no way it could be done. And her mother had said she was growing up! What is a lie, Mr. Ricci? Hah! If you have parents, you find out pretty quick.

Chapter Twenty-one

Wednesday. Thursday. *Friday!*

Franny hugged her so hard that Madeleine almost came fully awake before her daughter darted from the room. "Don't forget to phone the minute you get there," she called. There was no answer. They'd gone over it all last night anyway, so Madeleine simply sighed, smiled, rolled over, and was asleep again before Franny hit the front door.

Friday, nine a.m. She tossed her overnight case into her locker and spun the combination lock.

Friday, noontime. She hung out in front of the school with Melissa and Susan. Jamie tossed a Frisbee with Elliot, Mark, and Jesse. She didn't look at him.

Friday, three o'clock. The bell rang and Franny Philips twirled four to the right, two left, once around and, click, eight. She grabbed her bag and knapsack and suede-fringed jacket from the locker and ran out of the building all the way to the Eighty-sixth Street crosstown bus stop; too many kids from the West Side School took the Seventy-ninth Street crosstown. She waited until 3:30 before she got on the bus headed east. Jamie boarded at the Amsterdam Avenue stop. They got off at Lexington and took the subway down to Bloomingdale's; then they walked up Third Avenue together and finally over to Second, to the supermarket near Ralph's apartment—the big

supermarket he said he never used. Ralph liked the
deli, where he knew all the countermen and they
knew him, and he knew what went into the shrimp
salad and they knew he knew and cared.

By four-thirty, they were ready: as ready as a
couple of midget jugglers on the lam could be. That
was what they looked like—two short fugitives per-
forming an extraordinary balancing act. Jamie was
carrying his suitcase, his books, and a brown paper
bag brimming with groceries. Franny had her overnight case, her knapsack, two books that wouldn't fit
in it sitting on top of a flat white pizza box, and a
six-pack of Coke.

Luck was with them, however. Just as they were
working out how Jamie could get at his keys, two
men came out of the apartment house, and Jamie
quickly caught the door with his shoulder. Franny
ran inside and pressed the elevator button with a
corner of the pizza box.

In the little mirrored entryway upstairs, they set
their parcels down and quietly removed their shoes.
Only when both pairs were perfectly settled under
the lacquered table did Jamie unlock the door to the
apartment. He pushed it open and waited. Franny,
arms full again, entered slowly. Jamie gathered up his
suitcase, books, and grocery bag and, after checking
the hall to be certain everything was in order, followed her inside.

It had begun to get dark. The apartment seemed to
glow in the early twilight, pinker than before and, if
possible, more magical.

"I'm so excited," Franny whispered, staring up at
the glass ceiling through the leaves of the white bird's
tree. "We're here—we're here—Oh, Jamie—" She
twirled to take it all in and then she looked at him
and exploded with joy. *"We're here!"*

He laughed with pleasure. It surprised her, and she realized how rarely he laughed, and it made everything right.

"Come on," he said, leading her to the kitchen where they began to unload the groceries. Jamie stacked the items on the narrow counter, and Franny put them away, deciding, as each item turned up, where it belonged.

She left the soft white bread (the kind Madeleine wouldn't allow in the house) out alongside the peanut butter. They both decided that refrigerated peanut butter was the lowest thing around.

The pink prepackaged bologna went into the fridge. The potato chips stayed out. The ice cream went into the tiny freezer compartment that was empty except for a pound bag of shaved ice, a couple of conical beer glasses, and a small plastic bag filled with grass.

The chocolate sauce stayed out. (It poured faster and tasted better when it was warm.) The pizza was a problem.

"Are there any cockroaches here?" Franny asked, holding the white box by its twine.

Jamie shrugged. "I think the snake and the birds would probably keep the ecological balance."

"What's that supposed to mean?"

"Not too many roaches—probably."

She decided to play it safe. The pizza went into the refrigerator. They could warm it up later. The Twinkies, however, stayed out.

"Can you cook?" Jamie asked.

"Scrambled eggs."

"We didn't buy eggs."

"And chocolate chip cookies," Franny remembered. "I learned the cookies in school and the eggs because my mother hates mornings."

"My mom took cooking in Paris. She's a gourmet. Except when she's on a diet."

Franny closed the refrigerator and looked at the rest of the groceries. "Why is this stuff all so *good?*"

Jamie thought about it. "Because of the preservatives," he decided.

"Hungry?"

"Not yet. Want to play badminton?"

"Is there a badminton court here, too?"

"No. Zen badminton. You know. Without a net."

She wasn't sure about that part, but she said yes and followed him into the living room. It was much darker than before. Jamie turned up the rheostat that controlled the Venetian chandelier, and the room sparkled with light again. He took a badminton bird from the drawer of a teakwood cabinet and two rackets from the cupboard space below. He gave one of the rackets to Franny, threw a hidden switch, and an AM radio station blasted through the trees, sending the aviary into a momentary frenzy.

They hit the badminton bird back and forth, unconsciously playing to the disco beat that thumped and pumped through the electric jungle. Franny looked up, following the flight of the rubber-tipped bird, just as the first drops of rain fell on the glass ceiling.

"Jamie, look—"

"Uh, oh," he said, shaking his head gravely.

Franny stared at the rain. "I can almost feel it!"

"Yeah. It leaks."

"It rained the first night I was ever here," Franny said somewhat dreamily.

Jamie shook his head. "That was a drizzle. This is a rain."

A thunderclap underscored his words.

"I love this place," Franny said over the noise of the music and the pounding rain. She looked at him. He was staring morosely at the ceiling. He looked like Jamie Harris, someone serious and sweet and special. "I love you, too," she said.

She wasn't sure he'd heard. He just glanced at her and said, "We'd better get something to catch the drips." But then his soft, solemn mouth curled into a shy smile and she knew he'd heard her.

They brought in some pots from the kitchen. Jamie laid them out strategically and, sure enough, within minutes there was a rhythmic tapping of water into metal.

"Let's eat now."

"Okay," she said.

They worked together in the kitchen and the dining room. Jamie lit the oven; Franny put the pizza on a sheet of aluminum foil. Holding the foil's edges taut, they maneuvered the pizza onto the oven rack. Jamie lit the incense in Ralph's meditation corner and two little colored votive candles which Franny placed on the dining table. She discovered a delicate sake pitcher, a miniature vase, and a tiny inverted mushroom-shaped cup designed to hold the potent Japanese wine. Jamie opened two cans of Coke. The sake pitcher held a little less than a quarter of a can. Still, Franny chose the little pitcher to pour her Coke into. Jamie decided to finesse the cup or glass dilemma, as well as the clean-up problem, by drinking straight from the can.

The dining room shimmered romantically in the light of the candles and the rainbow ripples of the aquarium wall, and they carried their dinner to the low table and sat, cross-legged, across from one another, leaning against the Japanese backrests.

Franny poured her Coke from the sake pitcher into the tiny china cup. She bit into the steaming pizza with gusto.

Rock and roll music, interrupted by occasional acne cream commercials and concert announcements, and the sound of rain pinging into the pots came through the paper-thin shoji screens that separated the dining room from the living room.

It was the best pizza she'd ever tasted.

"S'great," Jamie said, the soft cheese threading from his braces to the pizza crust in his hand.

"Did you really help Ralph build the fish tanks?"

"Aquarium. Yes."

She slugged down a shot of Coke and refilled the little cup. "Aquarium. Are you interested in—er—"

"Marine bilogy." Jamie supplied the missing words.

"Uh—there's—uh, this stuff all over your braces— pizza, I guess."

"Gross," Jamie groaned. He turned his head away from her and rubbed his teeth with his linen napkin. "Better?"

"You got it all," she assured him. "Is that what you want to do? Work with fish? Be a marine biologist, I mean?"

Jamie took a drink of Coke and, just to be safe, shot it around his mouth hoping to dislodge errant bits of cheese and tomato. "The trouble with being a marine biologist," he said, "is that there's no money in it."

"I have a trust fund."

"How much is it?"

"I don't know." She poured another thimbleful of Coke into the sake cup.

"What are you going to be?"

"I was going to be a nurse once, when I was little. My mom almost had an attack. She said girls can be anything now and I didn't have to be a nurse. I could be a doctor."

"Do you want to be a doctor?"

"No," Franny said quickly. "I don't want to be a mother either," she added.

Jamie pulled another piece of pizza onto his plate. "My grandfather's whole business is waiting for me. He says I shouldn't turn my nose up just because Ralph thinks he's too good for it."

"What is it?"

"You'll laugh," he said matter-of-factly. He folded his slice of pizza down the center and nipped off the triangular tip.

"I won't."

"Yes, you will."

Franny wiped her fingers on her napkin, then drew an X across the left side of her chest. "Swear," she promised.

Jamie chewed his pizza thoughtfully. "Cemeteries," he said at last.

She laughed.

"I knew you'd crack up."

She tried to stop but couldn't. "I'm sorry," she managed to sputter.

Jamie leaned back and closed his eyes lightly. " 'Let 'em laugh.' That's what my grandpa says." He opened his eyes. She had her hand over her mouth, but her shoulders were still shaking. He closed his eyes again. "He says he laughs all the way to the bank. Now he's building high rises."

"High-rise cemeteries?" Franny asked incredulously.

He knew that would get her. He opened his eyes and nodded solemnly. "They stack them up. In a building," he said with a perverse flicker of a smile.

Her hand was still across her mouth, but now her lips were parted in awe. She wasn't laughing. "Did you ever see a real dead person?"

"My grandmother. She looked nice." He really didn't want to frighten her. "I mean, she looked dead, but she looked nice."

She poured herself another sake cup full of Coke and sipped it pensively. "I would have had a sister, but she died. Her name was Katie." *Daddy and me and Franny made three.* She remembered Madeleine's words, and, suddenly, she had eaten too much pizza and it was cold and she didn't like it at all and the Coke in the cup was just warm Coke and it was stupid to drink it as if it were some exotic Japanese drink.

She went on quickly. "She died before she came home from the hospital. I never saw her."

"What happened?"

Franny pushed her plate away and leaned on the cushioned backrest. "There was something wrong with her heart. They couldn't fix it."

"That's lousy," Jamie said. Then he took another bite of pizza. "Did they cremate her?"

"I hope not," Franny said, shocked.

"I want to be cremated," he said.

"Why?"

"It makes sense. Ecologically."

"She has a little tiny grave," Franny said. She stared at the sake cup. "But I don't think they cremated her."

Jamie knew there was something wrong. Not even the driving beat of Meat Loaf blasting through the shoji screens could drive away the awkward gloom. "One thing about my grandfather's cemeteries," he said in a stodgy businesslike way, "you get perpetual care."

"After you're dead, who cares?"

"I bet your mother cares."

Franny blinked. "My mother—What time is it?"

"Why?"

"She's having dinner with my grandmother—"

"Seven thirty-three," he replied, looking at his watch.

"I promised I'd call when we got there. She's going to kill me—"

They got up from the table together. "It's quieter in the kitchen," Jamie said.

Franny bent to pick up her plate and cup. Jamie carried his Coke into the kitchen with him. "Phone's on the wall, next to the refrigerator."

She set her plate down in the sink and finished off the Coke in her cup. Then she picked up the telephone receiver. "Oh, God, what's the number? It's my grandmother! I *know* the number—"

"Look it up."

"Sshh," Franny said, trying to remember.

Chapter Twenty-two

Sylvia Strauss, Franny's grandmother, was what new feminists called a "found" woman. But Sylvia had never been lost. She'd known who she was before the women's movement announced who she ought to be: she was a woman blessed with intelligence, energy, a free spirit, and a straight back. Also a healthy portfolio of tax-free municipal bonds.

She had a few weaknesses, to be sure: a penchant for ritual (at the moment, this meant her second bourbon on the rocks before dinner) and for fable —true stories and bits of gossip which she tended to embellish, not because she enjoyed lying but because she disliked all things drab. She was a naturally creative woman who enjoyed life and found it more imaginatively stimulating and in need of color and texture than needlepoint.

Sylvia's relationship with her daughter was nearly a mirror image of Madeleine's and Franny's. Because there was genuine love between them, they were free to carp at one another. And because Sylvia hadn't Madeleine's day-by-day intimacy with Franny, she was free to adore her grandchild without reservation. Or guilt. Thus, she was the first to express her concern.

"Are you sure she knows you're here?"

"I told you. I told her."

Sylvia swirled the bourbon in her glass and the ice clinked; she toyed with the four strands of pearls that circled her neck, and they clacked against her lacquered fingernails.

"Even when you were at Smith," she said, "I knew where you were every weekend."

"I was with Paul every weekend."

"You were?"

Madeleine stood and began to pace. Sylvia took another fortifying sip of bourbon and put the glass down on its crystal coaster.

"Paul stopped by," Sylvia announced. "He said—"

"He wants Franny—"

"He said," she corrected Madeleine, "that it's the first time in his life he's ever lived alone. Isn't that remarkable? At home, there was his brother. They shared a room. At school, he always had roommates and—in the army—"

"He wasn't in the army," Madeleine nipped the embellishment in the bud.

Sylvia squinted at her. "Sit down," she said. "You know, there's a lot of your father in you."

"We haven't been happy roommates for a long time."

"The bluebird of happiness, Madeleine," Sylvia warned, "is always greener on the other side of the fence."

Madeleine's mouth fell open, but no appropriate response came to mind. "Mother—," she said, and she heard Franny's voice, impatient and irate, closing the generation gap. She gave up, sank into the nearest chair, and smiled.

"What time is it?" Sylvia held her Patek Philippe at arm's length in a vain attempt to read the face of the watch. The telephone's ring was answer enough.

As she was closest to it, she picked it up swiftly.
"Francis?"

"Is it Franny?" Madeleine moved to the edge of her
chair.

"Grandma?" Franny said.

"Franny—your mother was worried tō death."
Madeleine reached for the phone.

"I forgot what time it was," Franny told Sylvia.

"The important thing," her grandmother said, staring at Madeleine's outstretched hand as if it were a
scaly claw, "is that you're all right. You're in the
country?"

"Westport," Franny said.

"Well. That's almost the country."

"Mother—," Madeleine said gently.

"Now, don't forget, Franny. Wednesday I'm taking
you to see the New Guinea dancers—" She caught
and held Madeleine's eye for a significant moment.
"Even if it *is* a school night."

"I said yes," Madeleine reminded her.

"You will love the mud men. They are huge and
painted and they move very slowly—"

"Mother. She's going to *see* them Wednesday—"

"Your mother wants to talk to you, darling." She
clamped her hand over the mouthpiece. "She's fine,"
she beamed at Madeleine. "You worry so." She shook
her handsomely tinted silver blonde head in repri-
mand and handed the phone to her daughter.

"Franny? Grandma was beside herself. It was rain-
ing so—"

Franny listened for the pinging of water into the
kitchen pots. There was none; nor, she noticed, was
there the comforting patter of rain on the glass roof.
"It stopped," she told her mother.

"It stopped here, too. Is it nice there?"

"It's beautiful."

"Are *they* nice?" Madeleine asked, remembering her brief conversation with the former Mrs. Rat.

"Sure."

"Have you had dinner?"

Franny glanced at the stained pizza box and the curling crusts in the sink. "Uh—Jamie's mom is cooking. She learned in Paris."

"Good. Let me have your number there—"

Franny's eyes called for help from Jamie, who couldn't possibly know what she wanted; then they lighted on the phone and the number printed there. "It's 687-4321," she said. And then, realizing what she'd done, she bit her lip and closed her eyes.

"Just in case—," Madeleine said.

"It's Westport." Franny assured her.

Madeleine was writing the number on a pad next to the telephone. "That's 203—? The area code—"

Anna, Sylvia's maid, entered the living room. She was Irish and fiesty and, having been with the family for many years, she had picked up some of Sylvia's mannerisms and habits, among them, the custom of having a few drinks before dinner. She walked stiffly, balancing on a fine line between bourbon and good behavior.

"Dinner's ready," she announced, and she took the silver hors d'oeuvre tray and Madeleine's unfinished drink and left as erectly cautious as she had entered.

"Dinner, Madeleine," Sylvia said.

Madeleine held up her forefinger, signaling her mother to allow her one more minute on the phone. "Have a wonderful weekend and remember to say please and thank you—"

"Mom—," Franny said in the exact tone Madeleine had recognized herself using with Sylvia.

"Oh, and Franny—" Well, she was a mother and she *did* have certain responsibilities. If exercising them exasperated her daughter, well, tough! Nevertheless, she softened her voice and tried not to sound too nagging or cloying. "Please, on Sunday, don't be late. You know your father. He's picking you up at six."

Sylvia shook her head and sighed her disapproval. "Don't nag at the child, for goodness sake, Madeleine."

"Kiss," Madeleine said to Franny.

"Kiss—Bye," Franny replied.

"Bye, darling." Madeleine hung up the phone.

Sylvia finished her drink while Madeleine tore the page from the scratch pad and pocketed it. Relieved and smiling, she turned to her mother. "She has a boyfriend."

Sylvia rattled her cubes again. "Do you?" she asked directly. She stood and, not unlike Anna, walked tall and straight-backed to the dining room. Madeleine, absorbing the question, followed her.

"I should have listened to you," she said finally. "You said I was too young to get married."

The large dining room table was buffed to a high gloss. On it, reflected in its rich mahogany surface, were a handsome flower arrangement, two immaculately polished silver candlesticks bearing stately but unlighted candles, two dinner settings on lace place mats, and a crystal and silver bell with which Sylvia could summon Anna.

"Will you listen now? I said you were too young to get married. Well, you're too old to get divorced."

"I'm thirty-four—"

Sylvia raised her eyebrow.

"Five," Madeleine capitulated.

"Out there—so is everyone else." She opened the door to the kitchen where Anna was finishing Madeleine's drink. "We're here, Anna—"

Chapter Twenty-three

Jamie had finished setting up the portable movie screen in the living room. He was threading the sixteen-millimeter projector. "You gave her this number."

"But I said Westport and she said 203 and—oh, Jamie—"

"Forget it. We're not going to answer it anyway."

"What's next?" she asked, relieved.

"More of me. Ralph's been making movies of me since I was born—" He started the film.

"That's not you."

There was a close shot of an elderly man talking with Ralph and a pert redhead. "That's my grandfather."

"And your mom. You look like her."

"Yeah. That's what everyone says."

The camera followed Jamie's grandfather as he walked down the lawn behind a luxurious-looking house.

"We used to go up there weekends."

"Westport?"

"Greenwich."

The elderly gent on the lawn almost tripped. "He's really a character," Jamie said. "See the dog? That's Tarzan."

"Tarzan?"

Grandfather Harris was saluting the statue of a

poodle. A live dog, frisky and tugging at his trousers, nearly toppled him. "And that's Jane. When Jane died—"

"Whoops—!" they exclaimed, and they laughed together as Jamie's granddad tried to pull free of the little dog.

"That's when he started the pet cemeteries," Jamie continued.

Suddenly Ralph appeared on screen again, clowning at the door of the guest cottage. "Hey, I took this—," Jamie said. The camera jerked from Ralph to a shot of Barbara. Jamie grimaced. "That was too fast."

"That's through a window," Franny said. "Hey, I see you—it's your reflection in the glass. You were taking pictures through the window."

Jamie's reflection was visible in the window glass. Beyond it, Ralph and Barbara were kissing, oblivious to their film-making son.

Franny turned to him. "My father doesn't take movies," she said. But he was staring at the screen. He wasn't listening. "But he takes slides all the time," she told him. "He even took me being born." She turned back to the screen. "It's gross."

Then she knew that she'd hurt Jamie without meaning to. She had hurt him, and what he was watching was hurting, too. And she didn't know what to do about it because he was Jamie Harris, the boy who never hurt.

He was watching himself watching his parents loving each other, and it had suddenly become more than a memory for him. It had become an achingly beautiful reality that would never, could never, exist again. He was watching himself as part of a real family, a whole family. And, mindlessly, she—thinking of her father's slides of her own birth; of herself as a shiny, slimy little creature oozing into the world—had said, "It's gross." Now she realized that he'd thought she meant his mother and father kissing.

Tentatively, she touched his arm. He stood up and switched off the projector. What he had seen still hurt, and for the first time someone else had seen his pain, and he was ashamed.

She followed him to the projector. She was shaking, and she didn't know why. And then she did know. It was because he had shown her what it was really like. Underneath the passive acceptance of certain objective realities—such as life, death, and divorce—he was, they were, helpless and hurting and, most of all, worst of all, children, which meant there was nothing they could do about any of it but try to hide the hurt.

Now that she knew the truth, she was scared. And she was shaking. But at least she had Jamie. He had had no one; he had gone through it all alone. She didn't know why, exactly, but she brushed away the fine straight hair at the nape of his neck and kissed the bit of flesh her fingers had exposed. She kissed the back of Jamie's neck, and it was almost as smooth and silky as his hair.

He flicked the rewind switch on the projector. For a moment, everything moved backwards. Ralph and Barbara were kissing again, still married, still in love. Then Jamie turned to her and she looked away from the screen and away from him. She looked down at her bare feet on the tatami mats, and then at his. Slowly, she raised her eyes. He moved toward her and she moved back and they were caught in the projector's light, their silhouettes showing on the blank screen. She looked into his eyes. He was waiting for her. For her judgment. He was utterly open and vulnerable. He was all that was left of the movie that had once been a family.

Jamie alone.

Franny alone.

She pushed the hair back from his high smooth brow. She ran her hand down his temple to his cheek and then to his lips, which were as soft as his braces were hard. She wondered whether she could kiss his lips without touching his braces. She needed suddenly to touch him. Her hand moved from his lower lip to his strong sweet chin, and with one finger she traced the vein that was pulsing along his neck. She traced the ridge of his collarbone down to the top button of his shirt, and she unbuttoned his shirt and he kissed her very lightly on the lips so that she didn't feel his braces at all and she didn't feel alone.

Chapter Twenty-four

Jamie was up early. He crawled out of the big water bed carefully, riding its easy ripples until he'd reached the edge of the sleeping pit. Still on his knees, he turned to stare at Franny. Last time, she'd awakened first. This morning, he was the one who got to see how she looked sleeping.

She looked, he thought, like a baby. It surprised him. She was wearing a ruffled, feminine, peach-pale nightgown, and her hair was very dark and wild across the pillows. But her eyes were closed gently and her lips puffed and slightly parted. She looked as innocent and soft as a baby, different in the morning from what she'd felt like in the night.

They had held onto each other all night long. First, their fear and sadness had drawn them together to seek solace from the reality the home movies had unexpectedly revealed. They lay locked together against night terrors that would not disappear in the morning—the nightmare of a family splitting like an amoeba from a single unit to separate organisms; the nightmare of floating lost and alone too soon, too young.

Then, they stopped being afraid. They began to feel, because it was impossible not to, flesh and bones bumping oddly, softly curling, curving piece by odd, sharp, and soft-edged piece against one another like a perfect puzzle. His knee socketed into the soft hollow behind hers. Her backside rested flannel soft against his thigh. His arm curled under her waist. He could feel the nodule of his elbow joint under her ribs, and her warm soft chest against his hard skinny one. And—for the first time—he liked his body.

For the first time, he thought it was going to be a pretty good body after all because it fit so warm and well against Franny's which was very definitely a wonderful, sometimes soft, sometimes strong and hard, healthy girl's body.

Jamie smiled down at her as she slept. It was pretty amazing, really, how she was a girl in the night and a baby in the morning and Franny Philips all day long. He tiptoed out to the living room where his clothes lay in a heap, all but the shorts he was still wearing and the shoes he'd left under the table in the hall. He dressed quickly and quietly.

The morning was overcast but dry. He made a list in his mind of what he had to get and where he had to go to get it. It wasn't much, but he wanted it to be right.

The streets were almost empty, but the all-night deli was open and he picked up a copy of Saturday's *Times* along with the cereal, juice, and milk he needed.

Franny was still asleep when he returned. He stripped back down to his shorts, opened one of the mirrored closets and found his favorite among Ralph's kimonos, and put it on. Then he went to the kitchen. He tried to work slowly, to give her more time to sleep, but the whole thing only took ten minutes.

The breakfast tray included toast, orange juice, Cocoa Krispies, and the copy of the *Times* folded to one-sixth its size. The tray seemed perfect to him. He carried it through the mirrored tunnel into Ralph's bedroom.

"Franny—" He stood above her with the tray in his hands.

She didn't stir.

"Wake up."

She turned over lazily and her body floated under the quilt on top of the rolling bed. He knelt down and, sliding the tray onto the bed, nudged her gently with it.

"It's morning."

She opened her blue eyes slowly.

"Surprise," he said.

"What?"

Her voice was startlingly deep. Then he remembered. It sounded like her mother's voice. Low and lazy. He grinned.

"Sit up. You have to eat the whole thing."

Franny blinked and obediently sat up in the bed. She stared down at the tray.

"There's no spoon."

"Oh, great," Jamie said, and he started back to the kitchen.

She picked up a piece of toast. "Or butter," she added. "Is there any jam?"

"I knew I'd forget something."

"And a knife. And a napkin. Please—"

"I don't do this every day, you know," he told her as he left the room. He returned with the utensils, the butter, and a jar of jam. She took them, or rather caught them, as he tossed them to her from the edge of the bed. Then he climbed down beside her, took the paper from the tray, unfolded it, and began to read.

Franny dropped a spoonful of jam onto the toast and offered it to him. He accepted, bit off a big corner chunk, and continued to read. She licked the jam off the spoon and started eating her cereal.

"I don't understand their problem," she said, blotting the brownish Cocoa Krispied milk from her lips.

Jamie turned to the sports section and grunted.

Franny shook her head. "I mean, being married is easy."

Chapter Twenty-five

Paul was glad Franny was away for the weekend. It would have been terrible moving out of the house with her around. He was glad that Madeleine had decided to take Shag for a good long walk, too. His hands were shaking and he stuffed them into his pockets as he watched the movers haul the last of the cartons into the double-parked van.

He had an inclination to walk once more through the house just to be certain he'd taken everything that belonged to him. But the inclination passed quickly, because he realized that what he believed had belonged to him was not his anymore and definitely not his to take. Walking through the place would only make things worse. Anyway, Madeleine would be back any minute and the movers were closing the van doors.

The Mother Truckers. That was the name of the company, and the moving men were women. Not mothers, probably. They were pretty brawny and very efficient and he'd liked their ad in the *Village Voice*. And, face it, there had seemed to be something appealing, just slightly perverse and poetic, about having women do the dirty work of breaking up his home—not to mention moving him into his new place, helping him set up his new life.

His fingers closed around the door key in his pocket. He figured he'd stick it through the mail slot, but his fingers were not lifting the key out of his pocket. They were gripping it so tightly that he could feel the ridges biting into his hand, and he could practically make out the word *Segal* imprinting on his palm.

He glanced down the street, wondering, and feeling like a jerk for caring, whether any of the neighbors were watching the great Mother Trucking exodus. He himself had witnessed two such moves in the five years they'd lived on the block. Saul Whitman had done it in shifts over a two-week period. Clair Michaelson, who'd left three children with her attorney husband, Alex, had driven up in her lover's BMW to supervise her movers. But no one appeared to be watching this morning. The street was almost empty.

He hurried up the steps and double-locked the black lacquered door and started down again, mindlessly slipping the key back into his pocket. Then he saw Shag, and then Madeleine carrying a Zabar's shopping bag full of groceries, walking toward the house. She was wearing the sheepskin coat he'd thought was too young looking for her. It looked terrific on her now, and he wondered for a crazy minute whether she'd gotten younger or whether the coat was aging gracefully. Then he saw her face and, if anything, she looked older than she had this morning, certainly older than she'd looked two years ago when he first objected to the coat. Her hair was pulled back in an elastic band and she wasn't wearing makeup. She looked— What did it matter? he thought. Hurt, sad, resigned, tired? Maybe she'd had to wait on line too long at Zabar's. Maybe that was all there was to the strained expression creasing her brow and pulling her full lips into a tight, unhappy line.

She was walking toward him.

"I took the pictures of Franny and myself," he said. He wondered if his voice was really quivering or whether it just sounded that way to him. He wanted to reach out and take the shopping bag from her. No, he wanted to reach out for her hand. He thought he should be happy that she seemed so sad and uncomfortable, but he wasn't. He wanted to hold her hand and let her know that everything would work out. Even if he didn't believe it. He wanted her to.

"Fine," Madeleine said. She stared up at him. Her big brown eyes were glazed, dead. She tried to smile.

"I left you the Billie Holliday records. And one of the Braque lithos."

"Thanks." She glanced at the Mother Truckers revving up.

"Well," he said, trying to lighten the mood, trying to make her smile or laugh or even groan with annoyance—anything, if she would just be Madeleine again and not the shrunken pale creature with the glazed brown eyes. "You won't have to complain about not having enough closet space anymore."

She nodded silently.

"I've got to get to my place before the ladies do. The Mother Truckers are okay," he said with the same false exuberance.

"I told Fran you'd pick her up at six tomorrow."

"I'm glad she's not here," he said. Then, "Oh—" He pulled the key out of his pocket and offered it to her.

She shook her head. "Keep it. For emergencies."

"Madeleine—"

"We'll settle things, Paul." She put her hand on his arm. "It'll all work out."

"Yeah," he said, giving in to his own pain and pessimism at last. With a half wave, he headed for the truck. Madeleine didn't wait for him to join the Mother Truckers in the cab of the van.

Inside the house, Madeleine followed Shag up the stairs. She moved past the "family" wall—the buff white wall that ran parallel to the ornate white-painted banister. On the wall were the outlines of the pictures Paul had removed, squares and rectangles whiter than the space surrounding them, somehow more real than the black-and-white photographs that remained—among which was their wedding portrait, hanging two ghost squares away from another family photograph. Paul had been scrupulous in taking only what was his. But a lot of what had been there was his.

She'd wanted him gone. And now he was gone. But how naïvely unaware she'd been of how much of her life he would take with him. There was an empty feeling in her stomach that echoed the empty look of the stairway photo gallery and the decimated floor-to-ceiling bookshelves. She turned into the bedroom slowly, trying to understand what had changed and how much was gone.

The sound of children in the playground down the street drew her to the bedroom window. She stared out blindly, some part of herself listening for the low, distinctive laughter of a seven-year-old Franny. Then, turning back to the bookshelves, she discovered a raggedy copy of *The Cat in the Hat Comes Back*. She had read it to Franny every night for about two months when they'd first moved into the house, when Franny had still been afraid to sleep alone.

Madeleine stared at the book and sighed deeply.

The book belonged in Franny's room, she decided with a burst of pragmatic energy. She walked down the hall, riffling through the familiar pages on which there were Crayola and Magic Marker scrawls. She was in Franny's bedroom, at the bookshelf, when the front door buzzer sounded. She tucked Dr. Seuss in among the newer paperbacks and texts, between a well-thumbed anthology of *Mad* magazine and a hardbound copy of *Charlotte's Web*. That was when she discovered *The Joy of Sex* stuck—obviously hidden—behind the other books.

Puzzled, Madeleine called, "Be right down," and, taking the illustrated sex manual with her, went to answer the door.

Steven Sloan, his hair still damp and smelling of health club chlorine, kissed her forehead and entered the house. He dropped his tennis bag into a corner of the hall, and then he noticed the book she was carrying.

"Brushing up?" he asked.

"Franny had it hidden," Madeleine replied.

He looked around. For years he'd been involved in and accustomed to the legalities of divorce. But now he seemed strangely awed, as if this were the first time he'd actually seen the immediate aftermath. He was smiling, but he looked bewildered by what his eyes encountered. Madeleine could sense the confusion behind his seductive grin, and it added to her own confusion.

"Come on," she said, feeling oddly sadistic or sad or just lonely, wanting him to share the oppressive emptiness she saw and felt. "Want a tour?"

She took his hand and led him up the stairs past the wall of photographs and white spaces. He glanced at the wedding portrait as she moved past it slowly,

still unable to look at it. She clutched the copy of
The Joy of Sex as if it were a talisman against the
disapproving power of the archaic photograph.

"I don't understand," she said to Steve when they
were in the bedroom. "I don't hide things in this
house. My God, Krafft-Ebing is out. *A History of
Sexual Customs* is out. Picasso's erotic drawings are
out—"

He looked around. "And Paul is—out," he said.

Surprisingly, he seemed almost as distressed as she
was. He took her into his arms and held her close and
tight and looked over her shoulder, through the
threads of her thick auburn hair, at the few records
lying where once there had been hundreds, at the
gap-toothed emptiness along the bookshelves and the
dust-free space where the stereo equipment had always been. He kissed her, and it felt like the first
time he'd ever kissed her—that scared and that tenta-
tive.

It seemed fair to her that he was feeling that way.
She pulled away from him. "Want some wine?"

"Yes, thanks."

She tossed the book onto the rug beside the bed
and went downstairs to fetch a bottle and two glasses.
When she returned, he'd pulled his sweater off and
was unbuttoning his shirt. He kissed her again before
she had time to set down the wine and glasses. She
thought he whispered, "I'm sorry, Maddy," when his
lips brushed her ear, but she couldn't be sure. Then
he reached past her and switched on the TV. She
heard a sportscaster's voice talking half and quarter-
backs.

Steve fell back onto the bed, pulling her on top of
him. She lay still for a moment, then bent to put the
wine and glasses down on the rug. Franny's book

was open, and she saw a number of hand-scrawled notes on the page that looked up at her. The first to catch her eye was the word *divorce* boxed in black ink.

She rolled off Steve and sat at the edge of the bed while he became engrossed in the football game. She picked up *The Joy of Sex* and began to read the entries at the back of the book. He leaned over, poured them each a glass of wine, and gave one to her. If he proposed a toast, she didn't hear it. She sipped the dry white wine and read Franny's strange list of dates and times and events.

"Steve—," she said softly after a while.

He stroked her back in reply.

"If you were a little girl who made up a mythical paradise called Shaggylon, would Shaggylon be West-port?"

He had no idea what she was talking about. "Your dog's called Shaggylon."

Madeleine stared at the dates and the word underlined in red. She finished her wine and then began to pace. Steve refilled the glass she'd left on the nightstand and held it out to her. She returned to the bed, took the brimming glass, sipped it thoughtfully, and then ruffled through a few scraps of paper beside the telephone until she found the phone number she'd jotted down at Sylvia's house.

She dialed the code and then the number. After two rings, the programmed voice of the operator was activated: *"I'm sorry. The number you have reached is not a working number. Please dial again."*

Madeleine's heartbeat quickened. Easy, old girl, she told herself, and dialed again. Two rings. Same message. She pressed the disconnect button and dialed Connecticut information.

"Directory information. What city, please?"

"Westport," Madeleine said. "Dr. Simon Peterfreund." Then she spelled the last name.

It was taking too long. She almost expected it when the operator said, "I'm sorry. There is no Dr. Simon Peterfreund listed for Westport, Connecticut."

A number of possibilities presented themselves. She settled on an optimistic combination of two: that Franny or she had somehow gotten the number wrong, and that maybe the Peterfreunds had an unlisted phone in Connecticut. He was a doctor. Perhaps the Westport house was his retreat. Surely he'd have a service number in New York in case of emergencies. She tucked the scrap of paper into her pocket, ran her fingers through Steve's hair, and stood up.

"I'm going downstairs. Want anything?"

He held her wrist; then kissed her palm without turning from the TV set. "I'll be down after this play. Anything wrong?"

"It's Franny—I—" She shrugged and smiled. "Probably not. I'm just going to make a few calls to be sure."

Chapter Twenty-six

On the Advent screen in Ralph's apartment, a college football game was in progress. Jamie, still in his father's kimono, was watching it. Franny sat beside him on the bed, browsing through a French photography magazine called Zoom and munching Pringles potato chips from a cardboard cylinder. She was not dressed yet either.

"I could call my mother," she announced.

"Why?" Jamie asked, not turning from the screen.

She thought about it another Pringle's worth. "Because—when my father watches football, my mother always calls her mother."

"Man, that is a run," said Jamie.

"Men," said Franny and shook her head and turned from Cornell Capa's war photographs back to the weird tranvestite series: "New York Unisex *vu (e) par Gilles Larrain.*"

On a small Sony TV, the game continued in Simon Peterfreund's office. Simon was stretched out on the analyst's couch in his workroom. Barbara, fresh from a bath and wearing a soft red robe, cuddled beside him. She patted the rise of his stomach.

"What do you think, diet or exercise?"

"Block, you rummies!" Simon called out.

Barbara stroked his stomach seductively. "Exercise," she decided, and she kissed him.

Simon watched the game and patted her hand affectionately. "It's almost the half," he promised.

At the half, Steven Sloan slipped on his shirt and went downstairs. Madeleine was in the kitchen with the school list in front of her and the scrap of paper from her mother's house. Steve had forgotten to bring down the wine. He went to the refrigerator and took out a bottle of beer as Madeleine began to dial the Peterfreund's New York number.

Simon picked up on the first ring. Barbara had fallen asleep beside him.

"Dr. Peterfreund?" Madeleine asked. She had expected his service to answer.

"Yes?"

"You're not in Westport," she said accusingly.

Simon sat up. "Who is this please?"

"This is Madeleine Phillips," Madeleine said, trying to keep the mounting distress out of her voice, "and my daughter, Franny, is spending the weekend with you and your wife and Jamie in Westport."

She'd blown it. She could hear the professional edge creep into his voice, trying to calm and appease her. He was used to dealing with disturbed people.

"My wife and I are right here, Mrs. Philips," he said soothingly, "and Jamie is spending the weekend in East Hampton—"

"East Hampton!" she gasped.

"And—can you hang on one moment, please?" He nudged Barbara. "What's the name of the boy Jamie's with in East Hampton?"

"Elliot Freeman," Barbara said, blinking herself awake.

"Jamie's in East Hampton—," Simon continued.

"Is something wrong? Did something happen?" Barbara asked quickly.

Simon stroked her hair reassuringly. "With Elliot Freeman," he told Madeleine.

Madeleine took a deep breath and stared at the Westport number on the paper. Steve came up behind her and kissed her neck. "Something is wrong," she said to Simon Peterfreund. "Terribly wrong. Fran called me last night from your house in Westport—"

"We don't have a house in Westport."

"She was with you. Your wife was cooking. The number was 687-4312."

"687-4312—," Simon repeated gravely.

Barbara sat bolt upright. "What are you talking about? That's Ralph's number."

Chapter Twenty-seven

It was late afternoon when Paul arrived. He asked the cabdriver to wait, ran up the steps of his former home, and buzzed twice. Madeleine was ready. She and Steve dashed past him and into the back seat of the cab. Paul climbed in front with the driver and slid open the partition.

"It's all my fault!" Madeleine cried. "You're right to blame me. I blame me. If you take her away from me, I wouldn't blame you."

"East Sixty-second Street," Steve told the driver. "Stop it, Madeleine."

"I already gave him the address," Paul said. "And you don't have to get involved in this."

"He'd take care of her," Madeleine said to Steve. "He'd know where she was—"

Steve squeezed her hand and leaned toward Paul. "We called, but no one answered. Then the line was busy."

"We?—What business is this of yours?"

Steve Sloan shrugged. "You never know. You might need a lawyer."

"I thought I knew her. Oh, God." Madeleine lit a cigarette. "Do you know what it's like to have a twelve-year-old child whom you think you know like the back of your hand—" She puffed rapidly several times before she remembered to exhale. Smoke from the cigarette obscured the tears that were starting to

brim in her eyes. "I don't know her," she said helplessly. "I don't know anything."

Paul's neck hurt from turning as he tried to face
her. He rubbed it vigorously as he spoke. He tried to
sound rational, in total control of his emotions and
capable of calming her, too. "I know one thing, Madeleine. It's not Fran. It's not our daughter. It's that
boy!" At the last sentence, his voice hit a hysterical
angry pitch and the pain in his neck pinched sharply.

Madeleine began to cry. Steven offered her his
handkerchief. Paul stared at the linen hanky and
then, with smoldering fury, at Steve. He started to
speak, but he winced instead.

"Need a couple of aspirin?" Steve said.

"Got any Excedrin?"

"No. But, wait." He rummaged in his pockets. "Aspirin and codeine," he said, producing a prescription
bottle. "Tennis elbow," he explained.

Paul accepted two of the pills. "They won't put
me to sleep, will they? I definitely do not want to be
groggy when we get to—to—Mr. Maserati's place.
Yeah. I want to be wide-awake for that one."

"Oh, Franny. My little girl—Paul, why? Why
would she—?"

"It's him, I told you. The kid. The little freak
who's so polite. They're the ones you have to watch
out for. They're the worst. I was a boy once. I ought
to know."

Barbara and Simon were waiting in front of Ralph's
building when the cab turned the corner.

"Girls that age, Simon—" Barbara was toying with
her white gloves. She hadn't taken them off. She was
just tugging at the fingers, then pulling the gloves

back up at the wrists. "Biologically, they're light-years ahead of little boys. They're manipulative. They're sex-starved." Her knuckles cracked. Why in the world had she worn gloves? And *white* gloves! Purity, innocence, racism—? *Guilt.*

"Barbara—" Simon tried to temper her tirade.

"It's her fault. All her fault! Oh, Simon. He lied to me."

As the cab pulled up to the curb, Steve said, "Now let me handle this—"

Paul whirled around. "Ow!" he yelled, holding his neck. "*I* can handle this." But Steve was already out of the cab. "It's my daughter," Paul called after him. Then he paid the driver and slid out.

"Dr. Peterfreund?" Steve said to Simon. "I'm Steven Sloan, Mrs. Philips's attorney."

"Steve?" Barbara said, surprised. Then she straightened the cuffs of her gloves demurely.

"Barbara?" He was wearing his boyish lopsided grin.

"I'm sure there's no need for an attorney," said Simon.

Steven Sloan's eyes lowered as he perused Barbara Peterfreund. "I haven't seen you since Caneel. You look terrific."

Barbara tossed her head. Her hair swung loose and free, picking up what highlights the late-afternoon sun had to offer. She patted it back into place. "I'm a wreck, Steve," she confessed with an incongruous smile. "I am a true wreck."

"Did you ever buy that little blender you wanted so much in Saint Thomas? Oh, do you know Madeleine? Barbara, this is Madeleine Philips."

"It was a coffee grinder—"

"Where is my child?" Madeleine demanded.

Simon had gone up and was now on his way back down the outside steps. "They don't answer the buzzer," he told Paul.

"There must be a super."

"Not on Saturday." Simon stroked his moustache. "We've called Ralph's secretary. She's meeting us here with a key."

Steve was grinning at Barbara, who was running her gloved hands along her hips. "I had no idea this was your son," he said.

"By my first marriage. I remarried." And now I'm wearing gloves, and a dress, and sensible pumps. From a string bikini to white gloves! But he was grinning at her still, and he seemed to be remembering the real bikini Barbara beneath her prim facade.

"It's a small world," he said.

"Why are we standing here?" Madeleine asked impatiently.

"We're waiting for Fiona," Barbara explained. "Ralph's secretary."

"The secretary. With the key," Paul told Madeleine.

She lit another cigarette, took two puffs, and ground it out under her boot. "Anything can be going on up there!"

"Actually," Simon said judiciously, "we have no proof that they *are* up there."

"Well," said Paul, "we know she's not in Westport—"

Barbara turned from Steven's gaze. "What's all this about Westport?"

". . . and your boy isn't in East Hampton. So," Paul continued, "where the devil *else* would they be?"

His anger drove Barbara into Simon's protecting arms. Paul took Madeleine by the hand and led her inside to ring the bell. "Everyone's a little high-pitched," Steve said to the Peterfreunds. Then, looking beyond Barbara and Simon, he saw an extraordinary pair of brown legs exiting from a taxi at the curb.

The legs were followed by an equally impressive pair of tightly skirted hips beneath a neat waistline and a flowing, voluptuously filled blouse that was open two buttons too low for anyone's comfort but the wearer's. The exquisitely high-boned face, rouged and false-eyelashed to something beyond perfection, was smiling through scarlet-glossed lips.

Steve whistled softly in appreciation.

Barbara didn't even have to turn around. "That's Fiona," she said.

"I got here as soon as I could, Mrs. Harris," Fiona said as she joined them.

"Peterfreund—"

"But I think you're wrong. I called and no one answered."

Paul came out of the house. "No one answers."

"I don't think it's right—," Fiona said.

Paul noticed her. "Has she got the key?"

"I'm Steven Sloan and I'm a lawyer, Miss—"

"Fiona. Fiona Tyler," Ralph's secretary introduced herself.

Steve beamed. "And Dr. Peterfreund is a doctor, and we're not breaking and entering."

She stared from one to the other. "I just have the key to water the plants—," she said hesitantly.

Steven Sloan took Fiona Tyler's arm and stroked it reassuringly as he led her up the steps. The Philipses and the Peterfreunds followed.

"He's going to have a fit, Fiona confided to Steve as she unlocked the door.

"I've got a feeling you can handle it."

She laughed. So did Barbara, who'd overheard the exchange. "Hah!" she said succinctly.

"What is it?"

"Nothing Simon—Oh dear, the elevator's too small."

Steve and Fiona were already inside, pressing the Open button, waiting.

"What floor is it?" Paul called. He was half a flight up already.

"Four."

"Right. I'll take the stairs, too," Simon volunteered.

"Darling—" Barbara's eyes moistened with pride and concern.

Simon winked at her. "Man cannot live by exercise alone." She blushed and got into the elevator.

"Steve!" Madeleine shouted. He tore his eyes from Fiona's buttons and pressed 4.

Paul arrived at Ralph's floor a moment before Simon and the elevator did. He saw and recognized Franny's sneakers laid neatly, side by side, under the black lacquered oriental table. Breathless, he picked them up with shaking hands and pressed them against his heaving chest.

"She's here," he told Madeleine. He'd started to say it softly, with relief and hope, but the sight of Simon helping Barbara from the elevator turned the words into a statement of aggressive triumph.

Madeleine took the sneakers from him. "Thank God," she said.

Not to be outdone in the caring competition, Barbara looked under the table, saw Jamie's shoes, and picked them up, too.

Fiona unlocked but did not open the door to Ralph's apartment. "You have to take your shoes off," she announced. Ignoring her, Paul pushed open the door. Madeleine in boots and Barbara in her little spiked go-everywhere pumps rattled through the hanging strips of film and strode onto the delicate tatami mats. Simon followed them inside. Steve, holding the celluloid strips back so that Fiona could enter first, waited gallantly. Once inside, he looked around and started to laugh.

"It's a Japanese geisha house," he said.

Fiona shrugged. "He was in the army in Japan."

Paul, Madeleine, Barbara, and Simon were halfway through the jungle.

"Fran—Franny—" Madeleine called softly into the relative quiet of melodic breaks in the thumping rock and roll beat.

Barbara dropped Jamie's shoes and covered her ears. Then, regaining her sense of purpose, she, too, called his name. They all paused at the hall to the bedroom. Then Paul, determined no matter what he might find, grimly led the way into the mirrored cavern. Madeleine set Franny's shoes down at the entrance to the hallway and followed him. The others followed her. Steve and Fiona were at the end of the procession.

Grinning and shaking his head in awe, Steve turned in the bizarre tunnel. He saw several Fionas reflected at interesting angles including a view from the top that confirmed what her loosely flowing blouse only hinted at.

"Do you type, too?" he asked her.

She laughed. "I type. I don't do coffee."

In the hallway, the music was muffled, but an odd mechanical pumping, a churning thump bridged by little watery gurgling sounds, became audible as they neared the entrance to the bedroom. The room itself, however, appeared to be empty.

Then Paul noticed Franny's plaid flannel little girl's shirt hanging on a glowing department store torso. He plunged ahead, turned right, and gasped.

Multiplied in countless mirrors surrounding the sunken tub, laughing and splashing in what appeared to be bubbling whipped cream, were Franny and Jamie, up to their necks in the whirling full blast of the Jacuzzi.

"Oh, my God—"

"Franny!" Madeleine shouted.

"Get out! Get out, get out—" said Paul.

The children turned, great smiles of laughter frozen on their faces, their eyes half bleary with soapsuds opened wide in bewildered disbelief.

They faced the group of gaping adults, angry and guilty, protective and concerned, amused and fascinated: Paul and Madeleine, Barbara and Simon, Steve and Fiona, respectively.

Then Franny and Jamie begin to sink slowly beneath the lather line.

Paul started up the steps toward them. Barbara grabbed him. "Don't you touch him!" she warned, wading onto the water bed. He tumbled down beside her.

"Get her out of there!" he ordered Madeleine as he tried to pry Barbara's white gloved claw from his suit sleeve.

Madeleine squeezed past him moaning, "It's all my fault—all my fault—baby—Franny—"

Barbara's heels dug into the quilt on the gyrating bed as she tried to achieve enough balance to stand without toppling. She managed a sort of knee-deep marching in place that played havoc with the quilt and threatened to puncture the bed as well. "How could you do this to me?" she shrieked at the hole in the suds where Jamie had last been seen.

Fiona leaned against one of the mirrored walls. "Like father like son," she told Steve with a hint of pride in her voice. And she blew a kiss at the life-sized portrait of a blissfully smiling Ralph, hands joined, bestowing serene approval on the chaos before him.

Franny, dripping a mercifully thick if patchy covering of suds, scampered out of the tub, and Madeleine quickly wrapped her in the giant bath towel she'd grabbed from the blue and pink neon rack.

"Now, no need to get excited," Simon said in his professionally soothing voice. He made his way to Jamie's side of the tub. "Just two children in the bathtub. That's all."

Barbara was wading through the water bed toward the Jacuzzi when Jamie, a bit blue from holding his breath for so long, finally surrendered and surfaced. He hauled himself out onto the slippery mica and Barbara searched frantically for a towel.

"Oh, Simon—do something!"

"Just remember, your body is beautiful," Simon mumbled.

Jamie found his own towel.

"Polite?" Paul pointed at him just as he began to wrap the towel around his waist. "Nice manners? Hah!—Does he look polite now? No! He looks naked, that's what he looks. Naked!"

Simon sighed deeply. Then he cleared his throat. "Okay, everybody, now calm down. Cool it—" He turned to address the children. Unwittingly, he started talking to their reflections in the infinitely confusing mirrored backdrop of the bath. Franny and Jamie had their backs to him and were trying to dress under their towels. They reached for their underwear, picked up the wrong pairs, and exchanged them as Simon continued.

"First," he told the mirror, "I want you both to know that we are not angry—"

"I'm angry," Paul growled. "I am really angry!"

He sat hunched at the edge of the bed, unable to look at the children.

"Will you let him handle this?" Steve said. "He's professionally qualified."

"It's not a crime to express anger," said Paul.

"He's angry," Simon said with great compassion.

"I'm hurt," Barbara whimpered.

Simon smiled tenderly at her, then turned back to the mirror, then turned again and found the children. "We know what you've done—," he began again.

"I don't!" Paul roared.

"What we have to explore is why—"

"I want to know *what!*"

Madeleine had gotten Franny's shirt off the glowing torso. She slipped it on her daughter now. "Why didn't you talk to me?" she asked Franny softly. "You know you can talk to me."

Simon turned to the adults. His tone was stern. "I know how you all feel. Now will you let me find out how *they* feel?"

"Oh, wow. That's heavy," Fiona said, impressed.

"You don't have to be afraid. No one's going to hit you," Simon told Jamie and Franny.

"I'd like to kill him," Paul muttered.

Barbara heard it. "Simon—"

He was still speaking to the children. "Everyone here loves you and cares about you—"

"Speak for yourself!"

"Paul," Steve urged, "will you shut up?"

"You keep out of this," he snapped.

"All right," Simon continued in his measured tone to Franny and Jamie, "you have dissembled—"

Fran, confused by the word, looked to Madeleine for help. "Lied," Madeleine translated in a whisper.

"We want to help, but we can't help if you're not open enough to share your feelings with us."

Paul jumped up from the edge of the bed. "I'll share my feelings!" he exploded. "That little creep slept with my daughter!"

"No!" Madeleine shouted.

"Face facts."

Barbara waded across the water bed again. "Take back 'creep'!" she demanded.

Paul ignored her. "Look at that bed," he told Madeleine.

She couldn't. "No—" She turned and began to edge away.

Suddenly Barbara was blocking her. Gloved hands on her hips, the shorter woman pulled herself up to full fighting height. "Your little tramp asked for it," she said.

Madeleine drew herself up. "You're talking," she hissed down into Barbara's face, "about my *baby!*"

"If you kept track of your baby—"

"What about your son?"

"He can do whatever he pleases—" She whirled away, her gloved fists shaking impotently. "He can do anything he damn well wants to do to her for all I care!"

"Barbara." Simon was shocked. "You don't mean that."

"How old is he?" Steve asked Fiona.

Barbara, stunned at her own behavior, turned abruptly. "I apologize," she told Madeleine.

"Jamie? He's twelve," Fiona said, shaking her head and grinning proudly.

"On second thought," Barbara said, "I mean it! Anything!"

"We are not being constructive," Simon announced.

Madeleine turned to Paul. "What can you expect of a child brought up in this environment?"

"I admit," Simon said to Barbara, "I had no idea this was where he went every other weekend."

"Now you know why I was always upset."

Loyally, defensively, Fiona spoke out in Ralph's behalf: "What's wrong with it?"

Simon didn't hear her. He turned to Madeleine and Paul. "This is not *our* environment. This is his *father's* environment!"

"Whose name she can't even mention," Madeleine said, "without calling him a rat—even to strangers!"

Barbara spun to face her. Then stopped and gasped. "You—you *rat!*" she raged suddenly, looking past Madeleine.

Madeleine followed Barbara's gaze to the bedroom doorway. "What did I tell you?" she asked triumphantly as Ralph appeared, followed by a breathtaking honey-haired amazon.

"What is this?" he roared.

Steven Sloan sauntered over to the newcomers and extended his hand to the woman. "Steven Sloan," he said, grinning boyishly.

"Anne-Marie," she replied. He was tall, and she was looking directly into his eyes. She only had to lower her lashes a little to do it.

"What's going on here?" Ralph demanded.

Franny and Jamie were standing near the tub, completely dressed now, completely ignored. They were, however, watching and listening intently.

"If you stayed home for a change, nothing would be going on here," Barbara accused.

He stared at her. "I just got off a plane."

"Big deal," Paul muttered.

Ralph's eyes widened further as he took in the devastation of the tatami mats. "Take your shoes off!" he demanded.

Fiona bit her lacquered thumbnail. "I told them, but they won't," she reported, anguished.

No one made a move to comply. "Who is she?"

Barbara said, having just noticed the statuesque addition to the already overcrowded room.

Steve put his arm through Anne-Marie's and walked her over to Barbara. "Anne-Marie, this is Barbara and—"

"Who the hell are you?" Ralph wanted to know, staring up at both Steven and Anne-Marie, and then staring down at Steve's familiar grip on the girl's arm.

Steve extended his hand. "Steve Sloan—I'm—"

"Get out of here," Ralph said, ignoring the hand.

"He's my lawyer," Madeleine said.

Ralph turned. "Hey," he said, recognizing Madeleine. He smiled. "Hey—how are you?"

"Lover," Paul said flatly.

Ralph took Madeleine's hands. "I really wanted to call you—"

"He's her lover," Paul said in a louder voice.

Franny and Jamie heard him.

No one but Steve seemed terribly concerned with the new information. "I can explain that," he said.

"I'm not asking for explanations." Paul turned to Madeleine. "Why *him?*"

"He *asked* me," she replied defiantly.

Franny took Jamie's hand. He looked at her. She nodded silently, and they began to thread their way carefully toward the hall.

"I was going to ask you out," Ralph was saying to Madeleine, "and then I thought, can I handle a real relationship?"

Barbara rested her head on Simon's chest. "I'm not angry anymore," she said. "I'm sad."

"I'm just between planes," Anne-Marie confessed.

"The fact is," Paul was telling Madeleine, "he's had something on the side all his life—"

She wasn't sure whether he was talking about Steve or Ralph. Neither was Ralph.

Simon stroked Barbara's silky red hair. "The sins of the father," he intoned. "Sometimes you go to the Bible, not Freud."

Ralph noticed the children making their way to the hall. Obviously they wanted out of this loony bin. Who could blame them? He winked at them, squeezed Jamie's shoulder as he passed by, and nodded, Hi, to Franny. Then he turned back to Madeleine.

"And if you think he's going to leave Pamela to marry you, you're really kidding yourself," Paul was finishing up.

"I'm in love with her," Steve declared.

Paul looked squarely at him. "Bull," he said. "I've known you for twenty-five years. The only one you've ever been in love with is yourself."

"I don't want to marry him. I never asked to marry him. The last thing in this world I ever want to be again is *married!*"

"You don't mean that," Steve said.

"I knew I should have called her," Ralph told Fiona.

Franny saw her sneakers at the living room end of the mirrored hallway. She picked them up and followed Jamie toward the lush garden where his shoes lay discarded. With both pairs in tow, they took their jackets from the closet and quietly tiptoed out of the apartment.

"Your wife called me," Fiona was trying to explain to Ralph.

"Wife?" Anne-Marie looked down at Ralph.

"Ex-wife."

Fiona nodded her confirmation to the girl and continued. "So I came over with the key. I guess they were shacked up."

Thinking she meant Madeleine and Steve, Ralph turned to stare in amazement at the couple. "Shacked up here? Why here? I don't get it."

Simon kissed the smooth bangs on Barbara's worried brow. "When you look around you, you have to say, how can you blame the children—" He looked around. "The children—"

"The poor children," Barbara cooed.

"Has anybody seen—" Simon began. Then he stood on the edge of the bed and shouted at the top of his lungs, "Where in God's name are the CHILDREN?"

Book Four
Facing Facts

Chapter Twenty-eight

They were in the vestibule tying their shoelaces. Franny straightened up and slipped into her jacket and Jamie looked up at her. "Wow—," he said. It was the first thing either of them had said since their escape from Shaggylon.

"Wow," Franny responded flatly.

It was evening now. The East Sixties were thick with Saturday night crowds, and Third Avenue was lit up like a carnival alley. Without speaking, they decided to head away from the last-minute Alexander's, Bloomingdale's, and schlock to chic boutique shoppers, away from the glaring movie theater marquees where crowds were already queuing up for the next show. They walked toward the darker, quieter uptown streets.

"I'm sorry about the mistake," Jamie said.

"About what?"

"The equation. The unknown quotient," he said thoughtfully. He glanced at her. She looked tired. Or sad. Probably both, he decided. "I didn't think X would be another man."

"Uncle Steve," she said in her husky voice. "Oh, boy."

He tried to cheer her. "At least he's a friend of the family. I didn't know Simon from Adam."

Franny stared at him for a minute, then she smiled gratefully. She put her hand through his arm and leaned her head against his shoulder.

He started to stroke her hair until he remembered that Simon did that to Barbara lots. He decided he didn't want to do it. Simon was okay, but he treated Barbara like a big baby sometimes. Franny wasn't a baby. It was all right for her to lean on his shoulder. In fact, very gently, so you could hardly notice, he leaned back toward her so that they were walking together, leaning on each other.

"Are you mad at your mother?" he asked.

She shrugged. "Steve's okay. I don't think she loves him though. Not like—"

He nodded. "Yeah. I don't think my mother loves Simon either. I mean, she does. But not like she used to love Ralph."

Franny remembered the movies of Ralph and Barbara kissing. She squeezed Jamie's arm encouragingly. "He likes you. Simon, I mean. He's just not too good with kids. Like he doesn't know how to be himself around them. At least that's what it felt like when he was trying to talk to us. He was trying real hard —and he wasn't really mad at you. He's just not— well, he's not Ralph is all."

"He was talking to the mirror," Jamie said, laughing suddenly.

"Oh, God—" Franny started to giggle. "I was so scared. I thought he'd find out it was the mirror and then he'd really get mad. They do that when they've made a mistake in front of you. They get mad at you."

Jamie glanced at her. "That's true," he said. "I never thought about that."

Franny took the implied compliment silently, with a smile. "Boy, I never saw my father so mad."

"Maybe there is another woman then. There's always the guilt factor to be considered."

"Oh, Jamie," she groaned. "Not another algebra lesson. Not tonight, please."

"Okay. It's your divorce."

"Anyway, I can tell—He doesn't want anything to change, you see. My mom is growing and changing and my dad wants everything to be like it was—"

"What's so terrible about that?"

He sounded as if he'd taken it personally; as if he thought she was talking about him and the pictures of the way things used to be. "It's not terrible," she said, thinking about it for a careful moment. "It's just that—well, nothing's like that, Jamie. Nothing stays the same. Ever."

He gave her that look again. "I think you're right. You know what else?"

She shook her head, no.

It seemed very hard for him to say whatever it was that he wanted to tell her. "I won't tell." She crossed her heart. "Swear."

He looked away, into a store window, and saw his face reflected in the darkened glass. He looked almost angry. "Ralph was really asking for it. I love him, but he blew it. He could have stayed married if he really cared. He could have if he really wanted a family. I love him, but sometimes I get mad and I think, How could he have done that to me? I know it's stupid—and selfish, but that's how I feel. I think he knows it, too—sometimes."

"He's fun but he's kind of—young, you know."

"Do I know?" Jamie gave a snort of derision. "I mean when you talk about someone who doesn't want anything to change—you are definitely talking about my father."

"You know, that's the first time you ever called him that."

"What?"

" 'My father,' instead of Ralph."

"Yeah?" Jamie scuffed his shoe along the sidewalk. "Yeah, I guess so. I haven't for a long time, anyway."

"Maybe you should. I mean, Ralph is what you call a friend. You know, a buddy. And I know he's your buddy and all, but maybe he could be a little more your father if you wanted him to be."

"Maybe. Anyway, I'm not sure I do anymore. I mean I just think of him as Ralph."

"You sound angry."

"Oh, come on—"

"Well, you do."

"I don't get angry," he announced arrogantly.

"Pardon me, Jamie Harris. I forgot that you're just so together you don't *need* to get angry or sad, or to cry or—"

Jamie laughed.

"What?" Franny asked.

"I was going to sock you. Honest. Look at my hand."

He was still holding her arm with his left hand, but his right was balled up into a fist.

"No, you don't get angry." Franny laughed.

Chapter Twenty-nine

They took the crosstown bus west at Seventy-ninth Street. Sitting in the neon glow and staring out at the tree branches that overhung the stone-walled transverse through Central Park, they lapsed into an uneasy silence. Finally, as the bus stopped for a light at Central Park West, Franny said, "What are they going to do to us?"

Jamie's head was resting against the cool window. He sat up, surprised at the question. Hadn't she ever been in trouble before? "Nothing," he told her.

She shook her head. "They will."

"No, they won't."

"They have to," she said logically.

He thought about it. "Well, they'll take away privileges, maybe."

"Like what?"

"TV."

"I don't watch it that much," Franny said.

"Cut your allowance."

"I don't get one."

"Not any?"

"You get more that way," she said. "They forget."

Jamie peered out the window again. He said something, but it was too mumbled for Franny to hear.

"What?"

"They'll probably tell us we can't see each other," he repeated.

"No."

Then they were quiet. The bus pulled up to the last stop on West End Avenue, just across the street from the West Side School.

"Come on," Jamie said. "We're here."

They got off and, although it was a block out of the way, they crossed to the school and stood and stared up at the strangely quiet building.

"They can't stop us seeing each other here," Jamie said.

Franny shuddered. She took his hand. "What if they make us change schools?"

"They won't," he said dully. She stared at him, still uncertain, waiting. "They paid for the term," he reminded her. "Come on, we'd better go now."

All the way to Franny's house, she kept thinking about the punishment. She thought about every privilege she had, and there was nothing to equal their crime. Then, as they approached the brownstone on Seventy-fourth Street, a new and terrible thought came to her. She knew what it would be for Jamie, and she knew she shouldn't mention it, but she had to. Very softly, she said, "Shaggylon."

His jaw set. It was as if, being near home again, he'd reverted to Jamie Harris, West—the boy who never hurt. "No," he said with finality.

"Not ever?"

He scowled at her. "Forget it," he said.

"It's not fair."

"They don't have to be fair. They're parents."

Franny wanted to take his hand again, but she knew he'd pull it away. "Why don't they just put us up for adoption?" she said bitterly.

"Who'd take us? We cost a fortune."

They walked up the front steps of the Philips house and stopped at the landing.

"I've got to go," Jamie said. Then he sat down on the stoop.

"Will you go straight home?"

"Why?"

"I don't want you to run away again."

"I was a little kid then."

Franny took her key from around her neck. Then she sat down too.

"Why were they so upset?"

"I guess because we're okay and they're all messed up."

"Why can't they be like us—"

"Someday we'll figure it out," Jamie said.

She thought about it. She thought about their walk uptown. "No. We won't," she decided.

"Why not?"

"Because nothing stays the same. Because we'll grow up, and then we'll get messed up, just like them."

She stood and walked slowly up the few steps to the front door. Jamie sat watching her as she put the key in the lock.

"Franny—"

"What?" she asked, opening the door without looking at him.

"It was the best sleep-over I ever had."

She turned toward him, but he looked off into the greenish glow of the streetlamp.

"Make sure you lock the door," he cautioned her.

He waited till he heard two locks being bolted from inside, then he stood and took a handful of bills and change out of his blazer pocket. If he walked to Central Park West, he could get a cab and, probably, make it to within a block or two of his destination before his money ran out.

He did just that. He hailed a Checker, gave the

cabbie the address, and sat back, not bothering to respond to the driver's small talk.

Ralph was alone when Jamie arrived. He was sitting on a couch staring up at the sky. The living room smelled of incense and grass, and Ralph was just taking a deep breath and slowly exhaling the soothing smoke from the joint in his hand.

He had heard the door open, and now he watched Jamie enter. "That was pretty dumb, James," he said when all the smoke had been released.

"Yeah." Jamie looked down at the shredded tatami mat. "They tore up your floor—"

Ralph patted the pillow beside him, and Jamie walked over slowly and sat down.

"How was it? Before they tore up the floor?" Ralph asked.

His face was totally at rest, his eyes dark; the panda rings under them seemed weighted with some new reality. Jamie stared at his father's face. It was, without the animation that usually kept his suntanned skin in constant motion, a very tired grown-up face.

"It was neat, dad," he said.

Ralph nodded, satisfied. He passed the joint to Jamie, who took it and stared at it for a while.

Chapter Thirty

Madeleine looked out the window of the taxi. She saw two children walking together. "Paul," she said excitedly, reaching for his hand.

With a good space between them, he was covering the left window while she stared out the right. He leaned across her as the two children passed under a streetlight. They turned out to be two boys.

She kept her hand in his. "Can we go to Penn Station? Or the Port Authority? We'll just look."

"Steve's right," he said, staring down at their clasped hands. "The best thing we can do is go home and wait." He was silent for a moment, then he sighed. "Why didn't I keep my mouth shut?"

"You couldn't help it."

"Feelings!" He spit out the word.

The cab dropped them at the corner. They crossed the street and walked slowly toward the house. Madeleine stared straight ahead, caught up in her own thoughts, shivering at the possibilities of what might happen to a twelve-year-old girl out this late on a New York Saturday night.

"Is Corine home?" Paul asked. His voice was strained, nervous.

"She comes back tomorrow," Madeleine said.

He squeezed her hand. "Look!"

The house was ablaze with light. There were lights shining on every floor. Together, they ran toward the door. Madeleine's hands were shaking. She handed the key to Paul, who opened the door quickly. They dashed through the living room and kitchen and met back at the staircase. They hurried up the stairs together.

Franny's door was slightly ajar. The light from the hall slanted into her room. She was there, in bed, asleep. Madeleine and Paul tiptoed in and stood next to the bed looking down at her. Shag whimpered and rolled off Franny's feet to lick Paul's hand. Madeleine brushed Fran's hair away from her forehead.

"Let her sleep," said Paul, scratching Shag's head.

Madeleine nodded and they left the room quietly.

"I'm so relieved I want to wake her up and— wring her neck!" Madeleine said once they were outside Franny's door.

"Sshh. You'll wake her."

Inside her room, Franny opened her eyes slowly. She rolled over, listened for a while, then pushed Shag down and closed her eyes again, happy, relieved, and very, very tired. She knew they were going to their room. The last thing she heard before she fell asleep was their footsteps, Paul's squeaking shoe leather and Madeleine's slow, sliding step, heading for the master bedroom down the hall. She was glad she'd decided to leave the note there.

Madeleine saw it first. It was a large piece of paper torn from one of Franny's drawing pads. "Oh, Paul—," she said, bending over the page. He came up beside her.

In large printed letters, with a black Magic Marker, Franny had written: *"I'm Sorry. I Love You."* There was no signature. Instead, she had drawn the face of a girl with long braids. And, with a red pen, she had drawn one tear on the girl's face. A red tear on the white paper.

"I love her so," Madeleine said.

Paul turned her toward him. She was crying. She reached out and ran a finger beneath his sunken eyes. He was crying, too. She hugged him then, grateful for his presence, for his sharing, for their daughter and their love of her. Suddenly the enormity of her relief overwhelmed her and she let herself hold him tightly and cry into the sweet-smelling collar of his shirt and she felt his arms tighten around her and she wanted to kiss him and did.

"I want to stay."

"No, Paul—"

"Yes," he said firmly.

In the morning, Franny, followed by Shag, peeked quietly into their bedroom. Their clothing was scattered in a heap next to the big bed. One of Madeleine's boots was near the door, and Paul's vest was under it. Her parents were both in bed, asleep, with their arms wrapped around one another.

Shag made a move toward the bed. Franny seized him around the neck and hauled him out of the room. Then she closed the door and they went downstairs together. She opened the front door and quickly dragged the *New York Times* and the *Daily News*, which were delivered each Sunday, into the house. She took them into the kitchen where they weighed down one end of the table.

She was sitting at the other end, eating a toasted English muffin and sipping her orange juice, when she heard Paul's footsteps.

The counter-top TV was on. She jumped up, shut it off quickly, and sat down again, looking past the comic section of the *News*, toward the door.

He came into the kitchen, fully dressed, buttoning his wrinkled vest.

She didn't even say hi. She said, "Can you move back now?"

"I don't know," he said. He seemed happy, though.

"Did you ask her?"

"No."

"Why don't you ask her?"

"She's asleep."

"That's the time to ask her," Franny said seriously. "When she's asleep she says yes to anything."

Paul wrapped his arms around her. "Franny. Don't lie to us again. Not ever," he whispered.

Tears welled in her eyes. She buried her head in his chest. "Don't *you*—," she said.

He thought of all those mornings she'd watched him and wondered and how much she'd gone through because he had been afraid to tell her—to tell himself—the truth.

"I promise," he said. "Say, you think you can make your old man some scrambled eggs?"

Chapter Thirty-one

Franny left the frying pan in soapy water and climbed the stairs to the master bedroom. Madeleine was still asleep. The room was dark. Franny climbed into the bed, settling herself in the rumpled sheets where her father had slept. She propped herself up against the pillows and poked her mother lightly.

"Can daddy stay now?"

Madeleine grunted.

"Promise?"

"No," Madeleine said softly.

"You're awake!"

"I was thinking."

"He went," Franny told her.

She nodded. "About you."

"He stayed all night."

"We were together last night because of you." Madeleine rolled over and reached for her cigarettes. Franny took the matches from her hand and lit one for her.

"Why can't he stay all the time?" she asked. She shook out the match and dropped it into the Wedgwood ashtray on Paul's side of the bed where he sometimes left his cuff links. It was empty, of course.

"He can't stay," Madeleine said slowly, blowing smoke into the air above their heads, "because you want him to or grandma tells me he should. When two people stay together, *they* have to want to—no matter what anybody else in the world says."

Franny nodded. Madeleine reached out and ran her fingers through the messy dark hair. She put her hand under Franny's chin and lifted it and stared at her daughter's face.

"You've got my hair," she told Franny. Then she looked into the beautiful clear eyes of her daughter. "And his eyes," she said.

Chapter Thirty-two

"That's what she said?" Jamie wanted to know.

They were crossing to Riverside Park. It was a chilly day. Most of the trees had turned from green to gold and several of them were already looking sparse-leafed and wintry. Miss Cohen had her whistle clamped between her chattering lips.

"That's exactly what she said," Franny replied. "That *they* have to want to—no matter what anybody else says."

Jamie nodded sagely. "She's right," he decided. "Are you okay?"

"It's cold. But I'm okay."

Elliot Freeman passed a red Frisbee to Jamie. "Get Cohen," he said. "See if you can knock the whistle out of her mouth."

Jamie turned to Franny. "You're an A, Franny," he said, straight out. He said it loud enough for Elliot and even Susan Metzger to hear. "You are definitely an *A!*"

Then he tossed the red Frisbee high into the air and Miss Cohen blew her whistle and they ran, laughing, across Riverside Drive all the way into the park.

ABOUT THE AUTHOR

H. B. GILMOUR's first novel, *The Trade*, was published in 1973, and was drawn in large part from her personal experiences in Manhattan's publishing world. In 1977, her Brooklyn roots provided authentic background for the novel (based on the internationally successful film) *Saturday Night Fever*. For *Eyes of Laura Mars*, a psychic thriller published in 1978, Ms. Gilmour combined personal knowledge of the "dangerously chic" contemporary Manhattan scene with on-location observation of the filming of the Jon Peters movie. Her latest novel, *All That Jazz*, based on the Bob Fosse film, explores the tumultuous life of one of Broadway's most driven directors. *Rich Kids*, based on a screenplay by another native New Yorker, Judith Ross, is set once again in a familiar milieu; this time, Manhattan's Upper West Side, where H. B. Gilmour currently lives with "a character who could have popped from the pages of this book," her daughter, JSG Sunshine.

TEENAGERS FACE LIFE AND LOVE

Choose books filled with fun and adventure, discovery and disenchantment, failure and conquest, triumph and tragedy, life and love.

☐	13359	**THE LATE GREAT ME** Sandra Scoppettone	$1.95
☐	10946	**HOME BEFORE DARK** Sue Ellen Bridgers	$1.50
☐	11961	**THE GOLDEN SHORES OF HEAVEN** Katie Letcher Lyle	$1.50
☐	12501	**PARDON ME, YOU'RE STEPPING ON MY EYEBALL!** Paul Zindel	$1.95
☐	11091	**A HOUSE FOR JONNIE O.** Blossom Elfman	$1.95
☐	12025	**ONE FAT SUMMER** Robert Lipsyte	$1.75
☐	13184	**I KNOW WHY THE CAGED BIRD SINGS** Maya Angelou	$2.25
☐	13013	**ROLL OF THUNDER, HEAR MY CRY** Mildred Taylor	$1.95
☐	12741	**MY DARLING, MY HAMBURGER** Paul Zindel	$1.95
☐	12420	**THE BELL JAR** Sylvia Plath	$2.50
☐	12338	**WHERE THE RED FERN GROWS** Wilson Rawls	$1.75
☐	11829	**CONFESSIONS OF A TEENAGE BABOON** Paul Zindel	$1.95
☐	11632	**MARY WHITE** Caryl Ledner	$1.95
☐	13352	**SOMETHING FOR JOEY** Richard E. Peck	$1.95
☐	12347	**SUMMER OF MY GERMAN SOLDIER** Bette Greene	$1.75
☐	11839	**WINNING** Robin Brancato	$1.75
☐	13004	**IT'S NOT THE END OF THE WORLD** Judy Blume	$1.75

Buy them at your local bookstore or use this handy coupon for ordering:

DAHL, ZINDEL,
BLUME AND BRANCATO

Select the best names,
the best stories in the world
of teenage and young readers books!

Bantam Book Catalog

Here's your up-to-the-minute listing of over 1,400 titles by your favorite authors.

This illustrated, large format catalog gives a description of each title. For your convenience, it is divided into categories in fiction and non-fiction—gothics, science fiction, westerns, mysteries, cookbooks, mysticism and occult, biographies, history, family living, health, psychology, art.

So don't delay—take advantage of this special opportunity to increase your reading pleasure.

Just send us your name and address and 50¢ (to help defray postage and handling costs).